DISCOVERY IN PASSION
Book One of the Passion Series
SHIELA STEWART

*Let the Romance
Captive your Heart

Shiela Stewart*

DISCOVERY IN PASSION
BOOK ONE OF THE PASSION SERIES
Published by Linden Bay Romance, 2007
Linden Bay Romance, LLC, U.S.

ISBN Trade paperback:
978-1-60202-081-8
ISBN MS Reader (LIT):
978-1-60202-080-1
Other available formats (no ISBNs are assigned):
PDF, PRC & HTML
Copyright © SHIELA STEWART, 2007
ALL RIGHTS RESERVED

The work is protected by copyright and should not be copied without permission. Linden Bay Romance, LLC reserves all rights. Re-use or re-distribution of any and all materials is prohibited under law.

This is a work of fiction and any resemblance to persons, living or dead, or business establishments, events or locales is coincidental.

Cover art by Beverly Maxwell

*To my sister, my best friend, Shelley.
You are an inspiration, and the proof that you can
always start over again and have it all.*

Chapter 1

Home sweet home.

Dear God, what had she done? No one pulled out a map, closed their eyes and pointed to a place to start their life. Let alone travel halfway across the country to a place you'd never heard of and knew no one. Only insane people did that. Was it any wonder her family had been concerned for her? She had definitely lost her mind, and she wouldn't be at all surprised if her mother marked this day on her calendar.

August eighth, nineteen eighty-three, Cassandra Evans loses her mind.

Yet, she couldn't be happier.

Standing before the tall two-story house with its white siding looking a little worn, the brown trim around the windows peeling and the lawn in desperate need of maintenance, Cassie was giddy with excitement.

This was her first home, and though it was small compared to her parents' home, where she had lived all of the twenty-eight years of her life, it was home. And honestly, what did she need a bigger home for anyway? She was only one person, after all.

Lifting the latch on the hip-high white picket gate, Cassie made her way to her new home. When the front door opened and a tall, goofy-cute gentleman in a dark navy suit stepped out onto the porch, she put on her best smile. And the reaction on his face at seeing her made that smile lift even more.

She knew what he saw, what everyone saw when they looked at her. More than once she'd been compared to Marilyn Monroe. Her naturally blonde hair curled in waves around a delicate face and hung past her shoulders. She had the same Marilyn sultry lips and the same dreamy eyes, or so she had been told plenty of times. But it was the body more than the face that every man saw and drooled over.

She was a full-figured girl who proudly liked to display her D-sized breasts in tight shirts, tanks and dresses. She didn't dress ostentatiously, but if you've got it, why hide it? And from the looks of the hang-jawed look of the man before her, he liked what he saw.

"You must be Steven Welsh. Pleased to finally meet you." Stepping up the three steps to the porch, Cassie held her hand out to the gentleman. His mouth still hung open.

"Uh...Cassandra Evans?"

"One and the same, sugar though I prefer Cassie." She took the hand he held out to her.

"You're early, not that that's a bad thing. I just got here myself."

"I believe in being early. Catch people off guard." She winked at him and actually saw his Adam's apple bobbing as he swallowed.

"Yes, well...would you like to see your new home?"

He was sweet the way he was blushing. "I would love to." He stepped aside to allow her through the door, and passing him she could see his cheeks pinken up even more. "Well," she said simply as she stepped into the small entryway.

The cubbyhole of an entry was adjacent to the living room, which was no more than twelve feet by ten feet. She knew from previous discussions with Steven that the brick fireplace had been renovated only a year ago. It certainly took space from the already small room. The walls were white; the floor was carpeted in a sandy brown.

To the left of the living room was a staircase in the same sandy carpet. Moving past the stairs, she walked into the dining room which was only a few inches smaller than the living room. To the left of that was the kitchen. An island separated the two rooms with counters in white and appliances in stainless steel. Her parents' cabin was bigger than this place.

But it was home.

"Those appliances are only a year old. The previous owners were remodeling before they left."

"Hmm," she replied while taking the stairs up to the second floor. The walls leading up were also white, and the doors and trim all in some sort of wood that resembled faux oak. To the left of the stairs was one bedroom no bigger than her closet back home; beside it was another bedroom of equal size. To her right was the washroom—and she was absolutely floored to find out it didn't have a jet tub. That would be remedied.

Entering the master bedroom, Cassie was surprised to see it was larger than the other two by a great deal, and also had a walk-in closet. She nearly snickered when she stepped inside and barely had room to turn in a complete circle. Whoever designed this had no idea what a walk-in closet really was.

And again, everything was in white and fake wood.

"I'll need a list of designers."

"Um...pardon me?"

Cassie shifted, her mouth curving in only the slightest bit of a smile. "Decorators. Who do you recommend?"

"Oh, well, there really is only one guy in town that does...some decorating. Actually, he lives next door. I could get you his number—"

"Or I could go over and see him. I like it," she said, turning to face him. "I really like it."

"You do?"

"Well, it needs some work, like paint, new doors, and the carpet needs to be removed downstairs. Aside from that, it's good. I like it." And it was a good thing because she'd already paid for it in full.

"Wonderful," he said on a long sigh. "Here you go."

She took the keys he held out to her, curling her fingers around them, and smiled. "You've been such a doll, Steven. Taking care of all the business here for me, finding the house and a space for my shop. I don't know what I would have done without you." She leaned in, simply because she couldn't resist making him blush even more, and kissed his cheek.

"If there's anything you need, I'm but a phone call away."

"I'll keep that in mind."

"What time are your things arriving?" he asked while walking back to the front door.

"This afternoon."

"Great. Well, welcome to Passion, Cassie."

"Thank you, Steven." Escorting him to the door, she decided to take a walk around her property and see what the outside had to offer. She waved to him as he walked away.

It was a warm sunny day. Stripping from her coral blazer, Cassie tossed it over the porch railing, kicked off her heels and walked along the sidewalk examining her yard. Dear God, she'd need to mow the lawn, wouldn't she? Why hadn't she thought of that before? And didn't flower beds need maintaining? Oh, wow, she hadn't thought of any of that. Maybe there was some kid in the neighborhood that would do it for her.

"No," she told herself. "You wanted this; you will take care of it." She mentally added a lawn mower to her list of things to pick up when she went shopping and hoped she could figure out how to work one.

The sidewalk led to the back of the house, which was actually quite large and boasted a two car garage. She had her work cut out for her if she planned on mowing all that grass.

Movement next door caught her attention, and walking towards the fence that separated her lawn from her only neighbor, her jaw nearly dropped to the ground. Standing on a ladder that leaned against the house stood a man in tight cut-off jean shorts and nothing more. His body was bronze and rippling with muscles. Lord, he had muscles. His arms, his back and even his legs. His sandy blond hair was long and tied at the back of his head. She

Discovery in Passion

felt the drool slide down her chin and did nothing to wipe it away.

Sweet heavenly God, the man was magnificent.

"Ex—" She cleared the lump in her throat. "Excuse me." *Oh, baby, look at those muscles bunch as he moves.* "Hi." She swallowed the drool about to dribble down her chin.

"Hey."

"I'm your new neighbor." And hadn't she hit the jackpot with him. Who could ask for a better neighbor than a god like that? "Cassie Evans."

"Welcome to the neighborhood, Miss Evans."

Those muscles rippled when he climbed down the ladder, and she actually felt herself moisten watching them. "Thank you. My stuff will be arriving this afternoon. I was told by my realtor that you do some decorating."

"Depends on what you mean by decorating."

Even his face was magnificent. It was long, sharp and damn sexy in those dark glasses that unfortunately hid his eyes. And the closer he got, the more she saw. His chest was firm, muscular and glistened with a light film of sweat. She was going to start drooling again. "I'm looking at having carpet removed and replaced with hardwood, doors replaced, maybe even windows and the entire house painted inside and out."

"Well," he swept a hand across his brow. "I do floors, I do doors, but I don't paint and I know someone who does windows."

Even his voice was sexy. Deep, low and a little scratchy. "Okay. Do you know who I could contact to paint my house?"

"I know a guy; he does interior and exterior. I can get his number for you."

"I would appreciate that." She shifted, suddenly feeling a great deal warmer than she had earlier. "I didn't catch your name."

"Because I never gave it. Thomas Healy, but everyone calls me Tom."

She held her hand out to him "Pleasure to meet you, Thomas." She winked, taking his hand and giving it a good squeeze before releasing it regretfully. Thomas suited him better. "Have you lived here long?"

Thomas hooked his thumbs through his belt loops, and she nearly sighed as they dipped just a bit lower revealing a thin line of hair from his navel down. If he looked like a god, she could only imagine what the parts that were hidden looked like. And if she didn't stop imagining it, she was going to embarrass herself.

"About five years now."

"Oh, you didn't grow up here?"

"Nope."

"I came from Calgary, so this is a big change for me." From big city life to small town living.

"I imagine so. Well, I need to get back to my gutters."

"Oh, was that what you were doing up on the ladder? Okay, I guess I'll see you around, neighbor." She cast him a flirty smile before walking back to the house.

~

Thomas waited until she was inside and had closed her door before he let out the breath he'd been holding. Holy shit, that woman had a body and then some. And that scanty camisole top she wore didn't leave much to the imagination. What color were her eyes? The hell if he knew; all he'd seen was that bod. The short skirt she'd worn had been unbelievably snug against a mighty fine ass, and as she'd walked to the house, swaying her hips, he thought he might lose his mind.

Shaking his mind clear, he walked back to the ladder.

Chapter 2

The anticipation was killing her. Standing at her front door—and that was still something she was getting used to, her house—Cassie waited while the delivery man walked up the path towards her. Having lived with her parents all her life, she'd never bought anything for herself aside from clothing, music or bed coverings. Now, not only had she bought a house, but she'd purchased furnishings to fill that house. Cassie thought she might burst with excitement.

"Miss Evans?"

"Please, call me Cassie." She wanted to jump up and down and scream with joy, but instead she simply said, "Is that all of my stuff?"

"Every last piece. My name is Mike, and I need you to sign here."

She took the clipboard and the pen he held out to her and read over the details of what she was signing for. Giving it a nod of acceptance, she signed her name and handed it back to the gentleman who looked to be at least fifty and slightly overweight. "There you go, Mike." She flashed her winning smile, knowing full well it always made a man sweat.

He turned, unaffected, and sauntered off to the van. *Can't win them all over*, she thought, watching another gentleman, this one younger, slip out from around the van and open the back sliding door. She couldn't wait.

Spinning around, Cassie mentally arranged where she would set everything up. The dining room table might be a tad bit too large, but it didn't matter. She had loved it the instant she'd seen it in the store. It was dark oak, oval, with beautifully detailed etchings along the bottom edge of the table. And the chairs were also in oak with fluffy black speckled seat covers. It would fit perfectly in the kitchen.

And in the living room, she would put the cream

leather sofa under the window beside the fireplace, so she could relax after work with a good book while the fire warmed her feet. She'd heard the winters were brutally cold in the prairies. The TV would go on the opposite wall and the chair in the corner. Oh, she simply couldn't wait.

Three hours later, Cassie was in her kitchen, unpacking one of the boxes that held her dinner set. This, too, was in black and white, and she thought how perfectly she had chosen things. She hadn't even known what the inside of the house had looked like when she'd purchased it. Feeling that black and white was the safest, she'd gone for it.

The knock on the back screen door made her jump. Guess she was a little jumpy all alone in her house. Laughing off her skittishness, Cassie walked to the door. When she saw who was standing on the other side, she beamed up at him. "Well, hello, neighbor."

"I thought I would run these over to you." Thomas held the business cards out to her.

Taking them, her nails brushed over his fingers, and she smiled inwardly, amused when his eyes flickered with a reaction. She knew perfectly well when men looked at her they saw a woman with huge tits and a stunning face. She'd been blessed with both looks and a killer body, and she loved to make men squirm with both.

"What are these?" Cassie asked, purposely dipping her voice lower to make it sound more sultry.

"My business card, along with a few people I think who might be able to help you."

"Sweet. Thanks." She could smell the scent of some sort of soap on him. Seeing his hair was still wet, she deduced he'd just showered. He'd changed his clothes, so instead of the tight shorts he had worn, he now wore jeans and a t-shirt. She regretted that most of his muscular body was covered. "Care to join me for some lemonade? I just made a fresh pitcher."

"I don't—"

"Oh, come on, one glass. I thought maybe you could fill me in on the town and what I have to expect. One glass," Cassie prodded on, refusing to take no for an answer.

"One glass, I suppose."

Smiling bright, she stepped aside to allow him in and as he passed she closed her eyes and drew in his scent.

"Looks like your stuff got here in one piece." Thomas said, glancing around the rooms.

Her eyes opened slowly, lazily. "You say that with surprise." Skirting around the large table, she walked to the kitchen. Placing the cards on the island, Cassie grabbed two of the glasses she'd already unpacked and filled them with lemonade from the fridge.

Thomas shrugged, leaning against the island splitting the kitchen from the dining room. "There's always bound to be something broken, especially in long distance moves."

"Well, I gave them plenty of incentive to make sure I got everything in one piece. Here you go."

He took the glass, glancing down into the yellow liquid. "Thanks."

"So, tell me about the town." Heading to the dining room chairs, Cassie sat down and slid her bare legs out, crossing them at the ankles.

"Not much to tell. It's quiet, for the most part. We're in the older section of town, so it tends to stay quiet. It's a little noisier in the newer section."

"Why is that?"

"The high school, mostly, and more younger families living there."

"You sound like you don't care for kids?" She sipped her lemonade, watching him carefully. He really was dreamy, and she could tell by the calluses and scrapes on his hands that he worked with them often. He was a hands-on kind of man, and she so loved a hands-on man.

Especially if those hands were on her body.

"Oh, I love kids. I just like my quiet time."

A man who liked his quiet time...he was getting better and better by the second. "Where did you live before coming here?"

"Mississauga, Ontario."

"Do you have family here?" Cassie asked leisurely.

"Nope." Thomas lifted his glass and drank.

"Why the move then?"

"Wanted to get away. You?"

There was more to his story, she thought, than that. "Came into a huge chunk of money, was told to do something with it in order to have it. Closed my eyes, pointed to the map, and here I am."

One sandy brow lifted. "Just like that?"

"Just like that. I bought a little shop on Main Street that I plan to open as a trinket shop."

"A trinket shop?"

"Yeah, doodads, collectables, dust collectors. Things like glass animals, crystal, bells, vases, ceramics, that sort of thing. I'll also be selling some jewelry."

"This is a small town."

"Uh huh." She spoke while lifting the glass to her mouth.

"Of two thousand people."

"Yeah, and your point is?"

"How many trinkets and jewelry do you think people will buy in a small town?"

"Lots, I hope."

"Well, good luck to you." He rested his glass on the counter. "So, show me around, tell me what you're thinking of redoing."

"Everything." She laughed, standing up and giving her short skirt a tug. "This rug, for one, has to go. I was thinking hardwood."

"Good idea. I do hardwood."

"Goodie." She rubbed her hands together as she led

him to the stairs. "I'm not sure about the stairs, but the carpet has to go here." She took the steps up, Thomas right behind her.

"They can be done in wood."

"Great. The hallway here has the same carpet which, of course, has to go."

"Wood," was all he said.

"I like your thinking. These doors—ew." She shuddered.

"You want all the doors and trim replaced?"

"Big time. I was thinking white."

"This is going to cost you a fair chunk of change."

She looked up at him with a sly smile, leaning one arm seductively against the doorway to her bedroom. "Honey, I have plenty to give."

He cleared his throat, swallowed. "Okay. I can write up an estimate, and you can decide if it is still something you want to do."

"I don't need the estimate; I want it all done. How long do you think it will take?"

He scratched his head. "We're talking several thousand dollars here."

"Uh huh."

He shoved his free hand in his jeans pockets. "Look, Miss—"

"Cassie."

"Cassie, I don't want to pry—"

"I'm worth two point five million dollars. I think I can afford it. If you would like a check upfront, I can do that. It's quite a lot of money, and I can give you whatever you like. I wouldn't expect a small businessman like yourself to have that kind of ready change."

He blinked several times, keeping his eyes level with hers. "As a businessman, I like to do things accordingly, and that includes writing up a proposal. If after seeing it you still agree to the terms, we can proceed from there, and—" he interrupted her before she could speak, "if at that time you wish to give a down payment, that is your prerogative. I neither require it nor need it. I have more than enough money myself."

She watched him turn sharply, heading back down the steps and wondered what it was she had said to irritate him.

"I'll have the proposal written up and back to you by tomorrow morning."

He didn't slam the door as he left, but she was damn sure he wanted to. A cool one he was, but she'd seen the anger in his eyes. Resting her glass on the table, she lifted the cards he'd left her and saw his on the top.

"Thomas Healy. Artist. Contractor." Her eyes went wide as the name stuck a cord. "No, no way. It can't be the same guy." *Could it*? Well, the only way to find out was to ask. Clutching the card in her hand, she headed out the back door and across her lawn. When she didn't see him outside, she figured he'd probably gone inside.

Lifting her hand, she knocked on the screen door. Through the screen, she could see into his house and into what looked like the dining room. There was only a table with four chairs. Shifting, Cassie tried to get a better look.

He stepped in front of the door and she gasped, her eyes lifting to meet his, then she began to giggle. "You surprised me." When he didn't reply, she cleared her throat and spoke, holding up the card. "It says you're an artist. Thomas Healy, as in *the* Thomas Healy?"

"That's what the card says."

She let out a breath. "*The* Thomas Healy who painted the *Lonely Mistress* and countless others?"

"Is this going somewhere?"

"Oh, my God, I can't believe I didn't recognize you. My parents have several of your paintings and sculptures in their house. They went to your show in Washington eight years ago, and my mother spoke about it for days afterwards. I've seen you in the papers. Wow, you don't look the same—well, you still look the same but not. The casual clothing threw me." Now she understood why he'd seemed miffed at her. He wasn't just any businessman; he was a famous, rich one.

"That's who I was; this is who I am. Was there something else you wanted from me?"

Oh, now, that was a loaded question. "What the hell are you doing in a small hick town doing construction and cleaning out gutters?" The guy was worth more than she was, and here he was acting like he was a normal class citizen.

"I like doing it," Thomas emphasized. "If there is nothing else, I have some things to do."

She'd insulted him. She hadn't meant to insult him. "Oh...right. I only wanted to confirm. Okay, so now I understand why you got pissy." Cassie giggled, shaking her head. "Man, *the* Thomas Healy, and he's my neighbor." When he simply stared at her, she cleared her throat and stepped back. "Right, busy. Okay...see you around, neighbor."

~

Thomas watched her as she walked across his lawn and back to her place. The woman had moves, and they were damn near hypnotizing. Shaking his head clear, he headed back to his office. His eyes flickered to the easel at the back of the room before shifting them to his desk.

He might have been a great painter once, but not any longer. That part of his life was over, had been over for four years, and there was no point dwelling on it. He enjoyed what he did now; enjoyed fixing things. Creating was in his blood, and he still did it, even if it wasn't on canvas.

Sitting down at his desk, his eyes lifted to the canvas, then down at the paperwork he'd been working on when he'd heard her at his door. He didn't need her distracting him, and she certainly had done that.

Damn, the woman was fine.

Shaking his thoughts clear, Thomas looked down at

the paperwork, his brow frowning. Before him, on the pad he'd been calculating on, was a rough sketch of Cassie. Putting the pencil down—he hadn't even realized he'd held it—he pushed from his desk and left the office.

Damn woman was distracting him.

Chapter 3

It was a little unsettling, being alone in the house—her house—the first night. She'd sat alone at her table during dinner time, eating a sandwich she'd thrown together from the supplies she'd picked up in Regina on her way through the day before. Oh, it wasn't the eating alone that bothered her. She'd done that plenty of times when she'd lived at her parents' home, but Cassie knew there had always been someone around, one of the staff at least.

But here, now, she was completely alone.

She'd turned the radio on because the sounds of the house creaking had begun to unnerve her. It was weird, Cassie thought, how much it had sounded like footsteps. She could have sworn at one point it sounded like someone had been running up the stairs. She'd shaken it off and had headed to bed.

The sounds hadn't stopped, so she'd resorted to leaving her radio going softly all night to dull the noises out. She'd finally dozed off close to two in the morning, only to have a restless night in her new bed.

The screams jolted her out of her sleep, and before she could recover, a loud bang made her jump. Her heart pounding, Cassie stared at her door, expecting someone to walk through at any moment. When the telephone rang, she nearly jumped to the ceiling.

"Jesus Christ almighty." Her left hand curled over her pounding heart as she reached for the portable phone beside her bed. Shaking off the creepy feeling she felt, Cassie answered. "Hello."

"Cassandra, it's Mother."

She let out a long breath and relaxed. "Hi."

"Were you still in bed?"

Her eyes shifted to the radio and the illuminated clock on the front. It was barely past eight in the morning. "Yes. Why are you calling me this early?"

"We didn't hear from you last night. Do you have any

idea how worried your father and I have been?"

Letting out another long breath, Cassie slid from her bed, completely naked. It was how she slept every night. "I am sorry, Mom; it completely slipped my mind."

"Well, darling, honestly. Didn't you think your father and I would worry?"

"Of course, you would; again, I'm sorry."

"You're safe, I assume, and in your new home?"

"Yes to both." She grabbed the silky robe slung over the bed post and slipped into it while shifting the telephone from ear to ear. Cradling it on her shoulder, she belted it up.

"I still don't understand why you had to move so far away."

"Mom—"

"You could have just as easily found something closer to home."

"Mom."

"Your father and I could have helped you—"

"Mother, take a breath." She did and Cassie continued. "That was the reason I moved away. I want to do this on my own, with no help. I need to do this." To prove to everyone, even her late grandfather, that she could do something on her own.

"Yes, dear, but still—"

Cassie heard the knock and gave thanks to whoever it was who'd just saved her. "I have to go, Mom; someone's at the door."

"Call me later and tell me how it's going."

Cassie walked down the steps, her bare feet silent on the carpeted rug. If she ran on them, would it sound anything like what she'd heard the night before? Shaking her mind clear, Cassie responded to her mother, making her way to the front door. "I will. Give my love to Daddy." She clicked the phone off, then opened the door and smiled up at Thomas. "Well, now, this makes it a good morning."

Discovery in Passion

"I got you out of bed?"

"No, my mother is responsible for that. She called," Cassie explained, holding up her phone.

"Do you always answer the door wearing practically nothing?"

She cast her eyes down the length of her body and the shimmering white robe she wore. She supposed it was a little…flimsy. "It's more than I had on before you came by." Her eyes lifted seductively to his. "To what do I owe the pleasure of your visit, Mr. Thomas Healy?" Cassie batted her long lashes as she smiled up at him.

He swallowed hard before responding, holding an envelope out to her. "Your proposal."

"Why, Mr. Healy, we barely know each other, and you're proposing to me." His brown eyes narrowed ever so slightly and made her smile even more. "Do you ever smile?"

"When I have a reason to. Here you go. You'll find it's very reasonable." Thomas gave the envelope a shake, indicating he wanted her to take it.

She took it but not in an ordinary way. She wasn't a flirt for nothing and slid her fingers along his hand slowly before taking the envelope. A muscle at the side of his left cheek twitched, amusing her. "Thank you. When can you start?"

"Don't you want to look it over first?"

"Nope."

He let out a long breath. "I can start any time you like."

"Today?" She was going to enjoy having him around all the time, ogling his fine ass and magnificent body.

"I can do today. What time?"

"Now."

"Now?"

"It's as good a time as any."

"Alright. I'll need to get my things."

"I'll probably be in the shower when you get back, so

let yourself in. Where do you want to start?"

He swallowed, shoved his hands in his jeans' pockets. "I'll rip the carpet out first. Probably would have been best to do this before you had your things delivered."

"I didn't know what needed to be fixed up before I got here."

"You should have seen that when you first looked at it."

"Yesterday *was* the first time I looked at it."

His brow lifted. "Get out!"

She shrugged. "I saw pictures, but you can never tell anything from a picture. Well, unless it's painted." She winked at him; the meaning caught.

"Okay, I'll be back in a few."

"I'll be in the shower." Cassie called out when he took the steps down from her porch. God, he was magnificent. Look at that ass, she thought, sucking in a breath between her teeth.

Turning, she saw the stain in the center of the carpet in the living room and frowned. "What the heck?" Moving closer, it looked dry, old, and deep reddish brown. She hadn't spilled anything on the carpet, and it hadn't been there the day before. Bizarre. Shaking it off, she headed up to shower.

It was a good thing the carpet was being ripped out today.

~

His tool belt hooked around his hips, Thomas entered Cassie's living room. He could hear the water running and figured she'd made good on her word of being in the shower when he got back. The thought of her in the shower, all naked and slippery, played a number on his system. Having seen her in that poor excuse of a robe minutes earlier was still etched in his mind. The cloth had been so thin that he could actually see the outline of her nipples through the fabric. And what a sight that had been.

Discovery in Passion

Giving his face a mental slap, Thomas moved further into the room and saw a stain in the carpet. Crouching down, he saw that it was dry and looked like it had been there for years. No wonder she wanted it ripped out.

But before he could get started, he needed to move some things around.

Thomas had everything moved towards the front door by the time Cassie stepped out of the shower. When he heard her taking the steps down towards him, he shifted to look at her and nearly swallowed his tongue.

She stood before him in a small swatch of a towel that had the same effect of covering her assets as a rubber band on an egg.

"I thought I heard you. Wow, you're fast."

He couldn't speak; he knew he had a voice, but it didn't seem to want to work right now.

"Okay, well, I'm going to get changed, I have to meet my realtor at my new shop. You'll be fine here by yourself, right?"

Speak you idiot. "Yes."

"Great."

He watched while she walked up the stairs, his eyes shifting away quickly when he caught sight of the bottom mound of her ass beneath the towel. Knowing he would get nowhere like this, he walked to the kitchen, ran the water good and cold, then stuck his face beneath it.

This was not going to be an easy job.

~

It gave her so much pleasure to watch a man swallow his tongue at the sight of her. Especially when she barely wore anything—and she'd purposely used the smaller towel instead of the bath towel to cover up after the shower. She'd wanted to get a reaction, and she'd gotten a damn good one.

Cassie dried her hair, putting in it in a flirty ponytail, then dabbed on make-up before slipping into the pale silky pink sleeveless blouse and black shorts. Cassie slipped her feet into the white high heel sandals, dabbed on some perfume, then headed down to see how far he'd gotten in her absence.

She found him crouched on the floor, pulling baseboards from the wall. "You are a busy bee, aren't you?"

"Better to get the work done that way."

He didn't turn to her, and she smirked. *Afraid I'm naked, big boy?* "I agree. How long do you think it will take to rip the carpet out?"

"I have a guy coming to help me, so…about an hour."

"A guy?" Cassie moved closer, standing right near his head, making sure he caught a glimpse of her naked legs and bare feet clad in heels.

"One of the guys I hire to help me on occasion."

Cassie crouched down now so they were face to face, not that he looked at her, though. "Do I make you nervous, Thomas?"

"No." He lifted his face and looked her squarely in the eyes.

"Hmm." Cassie didn't believe him for a second. "You're sweating. Want me to pick up some fans? This place doesn't have central air—and that's another thing that needs fixing. Know anyone?"

"I'll look into it." He went back to prying the baseboards from the wall.

"Great. Okay, I'll be about an hour. Help yourself to whatever you need in the house." Cassie stood and sauntered to the kitchen, smiling the whole time.

She made him nervous, and she would bet her millions on that.

Chapter 4

Since she had some time to kill, Cassie decided to take a tour of the town she now called home. It was small, but not as small as she had thought it would be. Main Street ran down the center of the town with the older section on one side, the railway tracks and the newer section on the other. It almost seemed segregated, but even the big cities tended to do that.

It seemed like a nice enough place, though she wondered what she was going to do without Reginald. She'd been going to him to take care of her hair for years. And from the looks of it, there was only one place to get your hair done, and she doubted very much that they would have the products she used on her hair. Well, Regina wasn't so far away that she couldn't go into the city once a month for a hair appointment.

Restaurants, there didn't seem to be many. Dear Lord, did that mean she was going to have to learn how to cook? Yeah, not going to happen. There were other means of eating, and Cassie made a mental note to pick up a microwave and some frozen meals while she was out.

Pulling her red Lamborghini to a stop at the curb, she slid from behind the wheel and noticed the eyes watching her as she moved around the car. New person in town was cause enough to gawk, but one that looked like she did, and drove what she did, warranted even more attention. And she was getting plenty.

"'Morning." Cassie spoke politely, heading to the sidewalk. The spot that had been chosen for her shop sat between a music store and the town office hall. She had the best of both worlds. Who wouldn't notice her shop? Then again, in a town this small, it was hard not to notice a shop; there weren't that many in the first place.

Spotting Steven inside the store through the huge glass window, Cassie opened the door and entered her business for the first time. "Hello, handsome."

He blushed. "Good morning, Cassie. How was your first night in your new home?"

Cassie was never one to not speak the truth. "Weird, scary and restless. Man, do old houses moan a lot."

"Oh?" he said nervously.

"I had to sleep with my radio on to drown out the noises. But I'm sure I'll get used to it in time. So, this is the place?" Cassie glanced around the tiny shop—a square really—and tried to think of it with shelves and ornaments and such.

"This is the place. When do you plan on opening it up?"

"Next month. I get my shipment of inventory next week, that gives me time to set up and get things ready. Know anyone who might be looking for a job?"

"I'm sure there are plenty of people who would want to work here. You could put an ad in the local paper."

"There's a local paper?" Her voice rang with surprise.

"Of course. You could also put up a notice at town hall next door."

"Sure. What was this place before?"

"A clothing shop."

"Didn't do well, huh?" The floor was a glossy, rust colored marble tile, and the walls were in a faint gray. Too dull for her tastes, so she would brighten it up.

"They were here for only two years before leaving."

"Two years, huh?" Cassie leaned against the counter. "Any bets on how long my shop will last?"

"Pardon me?"

"Oh, come on, Steven. I'm sure the townspeople are betting to see how long I'll last. Big city girl coming to a small town to start a business." Small towns were famous for their gossip and Cassie was sure she was—if not already—going to be the center of gossip, for a while.

"I'm sure you'll do fine, Cassie. Well, here are your keys." Steven held a chain with three keys attached out to her.

"I'm sure I will. Thank you, Steven. You have been a godsend to me." Taking the keys but not before sliding her fingers along his arm. She took great pleasure in making him nervous.

"If you need anything, you know how to get a hold of me."

She followed him to the door. "I have your number."

"Well, good luck."

"Thank you, Steven." Cassie flashed him a sultry smile, and once again, his cheeks glowed with embarrassment. He was rather cute.

She gave the shop a long, hard look after he left and her stomach tightened. "Holy shit, Cassie, what have you done?"

~

As she'd promised Thomas, Cassie stopped to pick up some fans. Though she'd been a little chilled during the night, she had a feeling the place was going to heat up with the warm days ahead the forecasters were predicting. Which was fine with her; she loved the heat, loved to lie out under the sun and let the warmth cascade over her body. And with it being nearly the end of August, she was going to take full advantage of the warmth while it was still around.

Maybe she'd sunbathe for a while after lunch, while Thomas was busy in her house. She couldn't wait to see his reaction to her bikini.

With her cart full, Cassie strode up to the cashier with a smile. "Hello," she said cheerfully.

"Hi there. You're new in town."

"That I am. I only moved here yesterday," she responded while unloading her cart.

"Well, welcome to town. Where did you move to?" the cashier asked as she rang in the order.

"Garrison Road. The house at the end of the street." When the woman's head jerked up and her eyes went wide, it actually made Cassie gasp. "You know of the place?"

"Everyone knows of that place."

"What does that mean?"

"It's a small town," she said simply and quickly rang the rest of the order through.

"Right." But the startled look on the woman's face told Cassie there was more to it than that. "Ever been inside?"

"No," she said hastily.

"Well, I'm having it redone. Replacing the carpets, the doors, painting it inside and out. It's not going to look the same when I'm done with it."

"Oh, it will always be the same house," she muttered. "Is that all for you today?"

Her brow furrowed, Cassie nodded. "Yeah." Paying the amount, she pushed the cart to her car.

It took her less than five minutes to get home, and after parking in her garage, she grabbed the two bags of groceries and headed to the house. Seeing the roll of carpet on her lawn brought a smile to her face. *Thank God, that ugly carpet was gone.*

Her heels clicked on the wooden steps to the deck at the back entrance of the house. Shifting the bags, Cassie pulled the door open and stepped into a huge mess. "Holy shit."

The table had been pushed against the island near the kitchen, and her sofa stood on end right beside it. The plush chair had been flipped over and rested on the table. She barely had room to enter. "Looks like he's been busy."

"He has and is," Thomas added, entering the room. "Pete and I are going to move your furniture out to the garage while we work on the flooring. Pete, Cassie," he introduced, pointing to his partner bedside him then to Cassie.

The guy looked like he was barely twenty. His round face was speckled with dust and beneath that were some pimples peaking through. His hair might be brown, but with the dust covering it, it looked gray. "Pleasure to meet you, Pete."

"Same here, ma'am."

"Oh, please, do not call me ma'am. That's for old ladies of which I am not. Call me Cassie. I have some more bags and stuff to bring in, but maybe I'll wait until you move the furniture out to the garage."

"Good plan." Nodding to Pete, Thomas grabbed one end of the sofa while Pete grabbed the other.

Since she had nowhere to go but outside, Cassie rested her bags on the patio floor, and held the door for them while they moved the sofa outside. Her mouth absolutely watered watching the muscles bulging in the arms beneath Thomas' shirt. She wouldn't mind watching him work all day. She let out a long sigh after he was out of ear shot. In no time at all, they had the furniture moved to her garage and her dining room back to nearly empty with only the table and chairs in it.

"I've ordered the hardwood, and it'll be here in two days," Thomas spoke as he walked past her.

"Two days?"

"It takes time to order that much in and have it delivered. And it'll give me time to sand down the floor boards and clean them before laying the hardwood down. That stain on the carpet went right down to the floor boards."

"Yeah, I don't know where that came from. It wasn't there when I first got here."

"Probably just didn't see it. "

"No, it wasn't there," Cassie insisted.

"That's the spot the Talbots were killed," Pete piped in, carrying a few of the bags from Cassie's trunk.

"Why, thank you, Pete. You didn't need to carry in the groceries."

He shrugged. "I wasn't doing anything else."

"What was that you said when you came in?" Cassie

took the bags from him and set them on the counter.

"Edward and Luanne Talbot were murdered in the living room here by their only son. He offed himself right after in his bedroom."

He'd caught her attention now. Turning to him, Cassie's eyes widened. "Someone was murdered in my house."

"Yeah...um...about ten years ago, I think; yeah, it's nearly ten. 1974. First murder suicide on the record for this town," Pete added, tapping a finger on his head. "It was a big deal; everyone talked about it for a long time. Still do, on occasion."

Cassie stared at him, her mouth open.

"You didn't know?"

"No, I didn't know." Murdered. In her home. She shivered. "Are you telling me that no one replaced that carpet after the murders?" Cassie shivered again.

"Oh, sure, it's been replaced a few times, but that stain always comes through. People say the place is haunted."

"People tend to gossip a lot in small towns. Are there more bags in Miss Evans' trunk, Pete?" Thomas inquired.

"Yeah."

"Maybe you should go get them," Thomas prodded.

"Sure thing."

"Did you know about this?" Cassie asked Thomas after Pete had left.

"I'd heard rumors. But only that, rumors. Small towns are full of them. I wouldn't worry too much about it."

"Oh, sure, easy for you to say. You don't live in a haunted house." Cassie looked around uneasily. Why hadn't she been informed of the history when she'd purchased it? Explained why the price was so low.

"This place isn't haunted." Thomas walked to the door and took the bags from Pete. "I've got a guy coming in tomorrow to look at the walls. He says he can have them painted for you the same day if you pick colors he can get quickly. I'd rather have the walls painted before I do the hardwood."

"You called a guy about painting for me? How sweet. Okay, that works for me. I like fast." Cassie winked at him, knowing full well he caught the sexual innuendo in her words. "I want the walls in aquamarine."

"Hopefully, he can get that for you."

"They're not hard to mix. I guess I won't be sitting in my living room any time soon. Hey, where did you put my TV?"

"In your bedroom. I figured you'd want to watch something while we fix up the place."

"You were in my bedroom?" Her voice dipped low and sultry.

"To put the TV in it."

Her eyes lowered and she smiled. "Uh huh."

"This is all of it," Pete spoke, entering with the last bag and a large boxed fan.

"Thank you, Pete. You are a sweetie." She took the bags, then leaned in to kiss his cheek. He was too young for her, but she enjoyed making him blush. "Would you boys like something to drink?"

Face flushing, Pete responded. "I'll take a rain check. I have to go to another job. Call me later, Tom, and let me know when to be here to do the floor."

"You bet."

"Bye, Pete. He's cute," Cassie added after he'd left the house.

"He has a girlfriend," Thomas stated, leaving the kitchen and heading to the living room.

"I have no doubt. He is a sweetie. Were you implying that I might be making a move on him?"

"It was only a comment."

The floor looked like hell, and she could see the stain in the wood. Shuddering at the thought of where it had come from, Cassie turned her attention back to Thomas. "No, it wasn't. You thought I was making a pass at him."

"It was obvious you were." He crouched down with his hammer and began hammering down loose nails.

She took offense. "Well, I wasn't."

"And the kiss on the cheek was nothing?"

"Yes. Sure, I like to flirt, but I wasn't making a pass at him. I'm more direct when I make my passes." She knelt down beside him. "Like this." Taking his chin in her hand, Cassie moved in for the kiss. She made it quick but definitely potent, and when she released him, Cassie could tell he'd been affected by it. "That was a pass." Leaving him with the taste of her lips on his, Cassie headed up the stairs to change into her bikini.

Chapter 5

Maybe it hadn't been such a good idea to agree to help his new neighbor fix her place up. If he had been a smart man, he would have given her the name of someone in the city to help her with her problem. But no, he had to be gallant and agree to take on the job. Well, he'd taken on more than he'd bargained for, hadn't he? The woman was getting under his skin and making him want something he'd been without for far too long.

Grabbing the sander from his tool shed, Thomas grumbled under his breath as he headed back to Cassie's. How was he supposed to get any work done when she was constantly around, dressed in those skimpy shorts or skirts, flaunting her assets for everyone to see?

You're stronger than that, Thomas.

He nearly swallowed his tongue when he stepped around the garage and found her sunbathing on a blanket on the grass. She rested on her back, and all that was covering her body was a few tiny swatches of material over those huge mounds on her chest and another thin swatch over her crotch.

Her skin was a glistening bronze and incredibly tempting.

"I can hear you breathing."

He swallowed—and was damn glad his tongue didn't slide down his throat—before responding, "You know there are laws against nudity in public."

"I'm not nude; I have something on."

"What you have on could not be qualified as something. There's barely anything there to be considered clothing."

She sat up, resting on her elbows, and tipped her head up to look at him. "Wait until I roll over. There's even less there."

"That might have been tolerated in the big city where you're from, but not in this town. You keep traipsing around half naked and someone's going to notice."

"It definitely got your attention, and I don't traipse."

"I have more work to do." She'd gotten his attention all right, and if he didn't get away from her soon, his attention was going to become very evident.

"What are you going to do with that?" Cassie called out while he walked away.

"Sand." *Don't look back, Thomas; whatever you do, don't look back.* He closed the door with a snap. Giving himself a few moments to calm down, Thomas walked to the stairs and plugged the sander into the extension cord, then flipped the switch. He didn't hear her come in, but the instant she touched his bare shoulder, his body tensed. Pivoting, he got a full close-up view of those beautiful breasts and felt his body rise to attention.

"May I pass, please?"

His mouth watered and was dry all at the same time. He wanted more than anything to reach out for one quick feel. Instead, like the gentleman he had been raised to be, Thomas stood to let her pass. And when she moved past him, he knew she purposely pressed against him because there was more than enough room for her to pass without touching him.

Damn woman was pushing him to his limits.

"I know you want me."

Her voice was like warm silk, and her blue eyes went smoky when she spoke in that sexy tone. And when her tongue slid out between those luscious pink lips, Thomas felt his control slip.

Giving in, he grabbed her arms, lifted her to her toes and took. Her breasts pressed against his chest when he held her close and as she breathed, he could feel them rise and fall. One quick yank and she would be completely naked, and he wanted that so damn badly.

The loud bang startled them both. Releasing her, Thomas stepped back. Looking down he saw the sander had fallen the two steps down to land on the floor

Discovery in Passion

beneath. Looking back up, he realized just what he'd been about to do. "I need to get back to work."

He took the steps down, and bending to retrieve the sander, saw that his hard-on was straining against his jeans. And...it throbbed something fierce.

"Work can wait," she knelt down to run a long tipped nail along his muscular arm.

His eyes lifted to the ceiling as the sensation sent shivers throughout his entire body. He was more than ready to give in, again, when someone rang the doorbell. "Better get that." Thomas wasn't sure if he was grateful for the distraction or not. Putting the sander down, he walked to the kitchen to pour himself a cold glass of water. He gulped it down, took a few deep breaths, checked to make sure his bits had calmed down before heading back to start sanding.

She stood by the door, a huge bouquet of red and white roses clutched in her hands and her face buried in the blooms, and he thought what a beautiful picture she made.

For the first time in a very long time, Thomas felt the need to paint.

"Secret admirer?"

"My parents." Her eyes lifted to his and he knew that would be the pose he would paint. *Sultry Innocence*, he would name it.

"How thoughtful." And staring at her was not going to get the work finished that needed to be done.

"They are so sweet. I love roses. The petals are incredibly soft."

He didn't look up because he knew perfectly well she was doing something with the roses that would only have a certain part of his now calm anatomy rising to attention. "Most flowers are."

"They've been very supportive of me. My parents. I don't know what I would do without them."

Great, now she was standing beside him, and one

look at those cute little feet of hers with toenails painted a fire engine red only made matters worse. "You're lucky to have them."

"I truly am. Oh, I know the perfect thank you." She knelt down beside him, and he felt himself harden. "Paint me?"

"Excuse me?"

"My mother is such a fan of yours. If I were to get you to paint me, she would simply die."

"I don't paint anymore." Thomas stood because he knew in the position they were in could be potentially dangerous.

"It would be the perfect gift," she spoke as if he hadn't. "And they would be the envy of all their friends. You have to paint me."

"I do construction now; I don't paint."

"Oh, please, you were born a painter. We should do it soon. Where would you like to do it?"

Here and now, but he wasn't thinking of painting her. "I only paint nudes." Maybe that would shut her up. He couldn't see her parents wanting a nude portrait of her.

"You do not. I've seen your work, Thomas. Your place would be best considering..." She swept her hand across the messy room.

"I don't have time to paint you. I have too much to do with fixing this place up." And if he didn't get out of here soon, he was never going to.

Cassie followed him to the door. "I won't mind if you take a break."

"I will." He shut the door on her protest and stomped off to his house.

~

"Well," she huffed, spinning around to head up stairs to change. She shivered at the sudden chill in the air, rubbing her hands over her arms. *Must be a draft from the fans.* But as she moved towards the living room, Cassie saw they weren't even plugged in. She tilted her head

Discovery in Passion

curiously, then shrugged it off and headed up to change.

She was going to find a way to make Thomas change his mind, one way or another.

~

He had that nagging itch that he hadn't felt in what seemed like forever. Pacing his kitchen floor, the picture of Cassie holding the roses in his mind nagged him to put it to paper.

He wanted so badly to sketch her, yet he was terrified he wouldn't be able to. He'd tried, oh, how he'd tried, over the past few years to create. But nothing had come to him, and Thomas feared he'd lost his gift when he'd lost his mother.

Yet now the urge to draw was stronger than he'd felt in a long time.

Giving in, he raced to his office and grabbed his sketch pad and pencils. Sitting on the sofa, his ankle resting on his knee, Thomas set the pad on his leg and began to sketch. It flowed out of him like water. His hand worked feverishly drawing Cassie's face, with its soft curves and innocent eyes. Beneath the make-up he knew innocence lay, and that was how he wanted to put her down on paper.

He drew her hair to fall over her shoulders and dip down to her breasts which were covered with the delicate blooms of the roses. He wanted to capture the sultriness as well as the innocence. And when he heard the knock on his door he simply called out, "Enter," and continued drawing.

"I have a plan," Cassie said, entering his house. "Where are you?"

"Living room."

"I'll let you paint me in the nude, but you have to agree to paint a portrait of me for my mother. Price doesn't matter."

"Okay." He rubbed the sketch, smudging the print to shade in her cheeks, speaking without thinking.

"Okay. Just like that?"

"Yeah."

"Well," She moved into the room. "What are you doing there?"

He continued to work.

"Oh, wow!"

Thomas stopped now, realizing she sat next to him, the scent of the roses drawing his attention. He looked up to see she held several in her hands. "What?"

She laughed, and the sound went straight to his loins. "Boy, you're really into it. I really like this; it could work as a gift for my mother."

He laid the pad down and let out a breath. "Fine, when I'm done with it, I'll give it to you."

"Great. So, where do you want me?"

"For what?"

Her brow lifted. "My portrait."

Thomas stood because being this close to her was incredibly unnerving. "I told you; I don't paint any more."

"You agreed."

"I did not."

"You did so, only moments ago. I came in, told you I would let you paint me nude if you did a portrait for my mom. And...well, since you've already started on that one, we should get started on the nude."

"I am not painting you in the nude, Cassie."

"Really." She placed the roses on the coffee table, then stood, releasing the string that held her wrap together and let it drop to the floor. "I say you will."

Chapter 6

Holy mother of God, she was a beauty. Even though he'd seen her in her bikini, seeing her completely naked took his breath away. She had faint tan lines over her nipples and a V over the silky blonde swatch of hair at the base of her vagina.

She was the most incredible woman he had ever seen.

"Would you like me to sit or lie down?"

Thomas swallowed the lust in his throat and reminded himself he was a professional. "On the sofa, lying down." And the professional in him wanted to get her down on canvas. He hurried without a word to his office and headed straight for the easel. Thomas hesitated, looking at the cloth draped over it and knowing it hadn't been used for over four years. He felt nervous pulling the cloth away.

Then the vision of loveliness flickered in his mind, and he yanked the cloth away. He hurried to gather what he needed, and carried it all back to the living room. Seeing her stretched out on his sofa nearly did him in. His dick actually throbbed.

"How's this?"

Good God, her voice was going to make him come. He set the easel down, and his supplies, then took a deep breath before walking to her. "Mind if I position you?"

"Oh, baby, do with me what you will."

Thomas hoped he could get this done without embarrassing himself. Her deep seductive voice definitely was doing a number on him. "Lie partially on your side."

"Like this?"

"Not that much; tilt your upper body to the side a bit. Like this." Oh, touching her had not been a smart move. Biting his lip, Thomas shifted her into position. "Now lift your right leg, bend at the knee and place your left hand across your belly. Perfect."

"Thank you."

He was going to lose it. Seeing the roses on the table, he picked them up and snapped off the blooms.

"Hey!"

"I'll buy you more." She'd brought over four, and he was going to use all four. Leaving one on the table, Thomas began plucking petals from the rest and dropped them onto her naked body. They fell lightly to land on her chest, belly and hands. The last bloom he took and carefully slid it into her hair just over her right ear. He took a step back, looking at her through a painter's eyes and was satisfied with what he saw.

"Are we good to go?" Cassie inquired.

With a nod, Thomas walked to the easel. Lifting the charcoal pencil, he began to work.

"How many nudes have you really painted?" Cassie asked while Thomas worked busily behind the easel.

"Ten."

"Wow. My nose is itchy."

"Don't move."

"Easy for you to say." She wiggled her nose, and he scowled at her. "Sorry."

"You only think your nose is itchy because you can't move. We haven't been at this long. I'll be done soon enough, then you can scratch your nose. Think of something else."

"How long will this take?"

He paused, looked around the easel at her. "We can quit right now if you like?"

"No. I'll deal with it. So, why did you move all the way out here?"

"Why did you?" His hand worked quickly, putting the lovely image before him on canvas.

"I pulled out a map, closed my eyes and pointed. When I opened my eyes, it had landed on Passion. Here I am."

His eyes lifted from his work. "You pointed to a map and that's how you chose where you'd live?"

Discovery in Passion

"You betcha."

She was an odd one. "Why didn't you stay in Calgary?"

"I wanted to be on my own, and I knew if I stayed too close to home I would only end up relying on my parents. It was time I moved out on my own in any case."

"You're what…twenty-three-ish?" Thomas spoke while his hand drew the fine lines of her figure.

"Oh, you are a sweetheart. I'm twenty-eight."

His eyes lifted now with a great deal of surprise. "You don't look it."

"You definitely know how to flatter a girl. What's your story, Thomas Healy? Why did you choose to live in this small out of the way town?"

"It was quiet." It was proving to be a little more difficult drawing her breasts than he thought it would be. Closing his eyes, he chastised himself for letting his mind wander, then returned to his art.

"It was quiet? What kind of answer is that?"

"A simple one. You moved your leg."

"I did not."

Thomas grunted, setting his pencil down before walking to her. "You're leaning it against your other leg." Taking her knee in his hand, he moved it back into place. His eyes drifted to the ripe pinkness between her legs, and he nearly drooled all over her. "Keep it there."

"I know you want me, Thomas."

Who wouldn't want her? "We can't always have everything we want." He proceeded to draw the detail of her body.

"Certain things we can, and I wouldn't mind one bit if you took me."

"I'm sure you wouldn't, but I don't mix business with pleasure."

"Fine, I'll hire someone else to fix up my house."

"You signed a contract which is legally binding."

She huffed. "Then I'll break it and let my lawyer deal

with the outcome."

"It'll be tied up in court for months, maybe longer, and you still wouldn't get your way."

"Why are you being so stubborn?"

"It's ingrained. I said don't move," he chastised her when she sat up.

"I nearly had you on the stairs at my house, and trust me, you weren't thinking of business or the damn contract at the time. I could have you begging me to take you. Just like that." She snapped her fingers.

"And you would only humiliate yourself. Lie back down," Thomas insisted.

"The hell I will." She stood up, rose petals floating to the floor.

"If you don't lie back down, I won't be able to finish the painting." He lied; he could draw or paint her with his eyes closed. Every curve of her body was ingrained in his memory.

"Screw the painting. You're trying to tell me that if I came to you now, wrapped my arms around you and rubbed my naked body against you, that you wouldn't take me?"

Thomas laid his pencil down because he knew he wasn't going to get anywhere until she was through with her snit. "Funny, you don't strike me as a desperate woman."

Her jaw dropped. "Desperate! How dare you."

"I believe anything worth having is worth waiting for. Anything that is rushed is not. I'm not looking for a quick fuck, and if that's all you're looking for, go hang out at the local bar and wait for the oil riggers to come in. They're always looking for a quickie." He mentally cursed himself for what he'd said.

"You bastard." Grabbing her wrap, she threw it on and stomped from the house.

"That was nice, Thomas, really fucking nice," he muttered after the door slammed with her exit.

Discovery in Passion

~

How dare he. Who did he think he was? She didn't throw herself at every man she saw. She wasn't some kind of floozy that slept with men at random. Okay, she was flirting with him, and she had made it blatantly clear that she wanted him, but she didn't do that with every guy she saw. She wanted him, and Cassie could tell he wanted her. So she'd thought, no harm, no foul.

Bastard.

Throwing the back door open, she stomped through the dining room and froze at the sight of the figure standing in her living room. She blinked, and it was gone.

Great, she was so angry that she was seeing people in her living room. Still furious, Cassie stomped up the steps, and then cursed at the sharp pain in her foot. Looking down, she lifting her foot, and saw the splinter of wood sticking out from her heel.

"Fuck." Pulling it out, Cassie hobbled up the remaining steps towards the bathroom. She caught the movement out of the corner of her eye, and when she twisted to her left, she could have sworn she saw what looked like a shadow of a man.

Hopping on one foot, she moved to the vacant bedroom and gave the door a shove. No one was there.

"Damn it." Returning to the bathroom, Cassie sat on the toilet, grabbed a cloth from the sink and dabbed it to her bleeding foot. "God damn bastard has me so furious that I'm seeing things. Well, I'll show him. Sometime he is going to come crawling to me, wanting me, and I am going to laugh in his face. You had your chance, big guy, and you blew it." Satisfied that the bleeding had stopped, Cassie left the bathroom and headed to her room to change.

He had some nerve.

Cassie grumbled under her breath while slipping into a black sleeveless tee and red shorts, still annoyed as she headed down the stairs to make herself something to eat.

He was a jerk.

Save us.

Stepping towards the living room, sure that was where she'd heard the voice, Cassie jumped when something skittered across the room. She yelped when someone knocked on her back door.

Heart pounding, Cassie stared into the living room a few seconds more, wondering what it had been that had scurried past her in a near blur.

It had been tall enough to be a person.

She jumped again at another knock. Sucking in a deep breath, Cassie expelled it before heading to the back door.

Her eyes narrowed as she looked through the screen door at Thomas. "What do you want?"

"I have a job to finish."

She kept her eyes narrowed and crossed her arms over her chest. "That's pretty presumptuous of you to assume you still have a job."

"Signed contract says I do."

"Talk to my lawyer." Be damned if she was going to give in and let him into her house. Not after he'd treated her so rudely.

"I'm sorry."

"What?"

"I'm sorry," he said, looking down, then back up at her. "What I said was rude and uncalled for."

"Are you only apologizing to get me to give you your job back?"

"I don't need the money, Cassie, but I enjoy the work. Most of all, I never back out when I give my word on something, and I told you I would fix up your place. I was a jerk, plain and simple."

Never say never. Cassie pushed the door open, allowing him inside. "Apology accepted. I was about to make myself a sandwich or something for dinner; can I make you something?"

"Why don't I spring for pizza? Peace offering," he

Discovery in Passion

explained when she tilted her head.

"They have a pizza place here?"

"And Chinese." Thomas laughed. "It's not that small of a town. Where's the phone?"

"Um…I don't know. Hang on; I'll check if I left it upstairs." Cassie took the steps in a sprint and found the telephone on her dresser. Grabbing it, she left her room.

She came to a complete halt when she spotted a shadow moving in the spare room. Inching towards it, thinking it was Thomas, she pushed the door open, and screamed.

"Cass?"

She took the steps in a dead run, nearly barreling Thomas down at the bottom. "Someone's in the spare room."

"Are you sure?"

"I saw him. Yes, I'm sure. We need to get out of here and call the cops."

"Stay here."

She gripped his arm, preventing him from leaving. "Where are you going?"

"To check it out."

"What?" Cassie grabbed his arm a little tighter, the pure strength she felt in the muscles astounded her. "You can't go up there."

"Don't worry about me; I can take care of myself." He pried her fingers from her arm and headed up stairs.

She stood at the bottom, her breath held, watching him enter the bedroom. The phone still clutched in her hands, she suddenly realized she had no idea who to call if they needed help.

"No one's here."

Her eyes shot up to him as he moved towards her "What? No, no, someone was in there. He was tall; he had mousy brown hair, kinda greasy looking, and he was wearing green coveralls."

"Well, I don't know what to tell you. There's no one

in the room. And the only way he could have gotten out was through the window, which happens to be jammed. I checked."

"He was in there; I saw him." She was sure of it.

"Did anyone come out of the room after I went in?"

"No."

"Case solved. There was no one in the room, Cass." He took hold of her arms. "Trust me."

Thomas released her, taking the phone before moving past her. Baffled, Cassie looked up at the bedroom. Someone had been in that room, and she had seen him as clearly as she saw Thomas.

Chapter 7

To her amazement, the pizza was actually pretty good. So far being in a small town wasn't too bad.

Because of the dust that had accumulated when Thomas had sanded down her steps, they took their pizza to the backyard deck. He'd grabbed two of her dining room chairs for them to sit on, and they sat quietly enjoying the warm summer evening and the delicious pizza.

"You've been awfully quiet."

Grabbing her glass of cola they'd received with the pizza, Cassie shrugged as he sipped.

"There was no one in the room, Cass."

"I know what I saw."

"Sometimes the setting sun can make the shadows in the room seem life-like."

"Shadows don't have eyes or hair, Thomas. Who lived here before I moved in?"

"A younger couple. Moved here from the city."

"How long did they live here?"

He shrugged, lifting his glass of cola. "A month, I think."

"A month? Why did they leave?"

Thomas shrugged again. "How should I know?"

"You didn't ask?"

"I like my privacy, and I give others theirs."

"What about before them?"

"Middle-aged man."

"How long did he stay?"

"Where are you going with this, Cass?"

She noticed he kept calling her Cass, and she rather liked it. Resting her empty plate on the deck floor, Cassie stretched her legs out before replying. "Pete said the house was haunted."

"Pete shouldn't listen to rumors."

"What if it isn't a rumor?"

"That's nonsense."

"Why is it nonsense?"

"Because haunted houses are only a figment of an overactive imagination." He stood, grabbing her dish and his before heading inside.

"Then why did the people who lived here the past year not stick around?" Cassie asked, following him into the kitchen.

"There could be plenty of reasons why." Thomas headed to the living room.

"Name them."

"You're being silly, Cass." He clicked the sander on, ending their conversation.

Maybe she was. Yet as she cleaned up the pizza and plates, Cassie couldn't help but wonder.

Was she?

~

She was being silly. The house was not haunted, and she was only seeing things because some fool had put the thoughts in her mind. She wasn't a jittery person; be damned if she was going to start being one now.

Shutting off the kitchen light, Cassie moved uneasily through the dining room. The house was filled with darkness, and she regretted not leaving at least one light on to guide her way. She hurried to the stairway, her body tense, her heart racing.

The shuffling sound behind her made her turn her head, and when she saw the shadows moving, she screamed and ran up the stairs.

"My house isn't haunted, my house isn't haunted, my house isn't haunted." Slamming her bedroom door, Cassie jumped onto her bed, and inched right up to the head board, curling her legs to her chest.

The boom of thunder rattled the windows and nearly sent her over the edge.

Panting, grabbing hold of a pillow, she clutched it to her chest, her heart pounding.

Discovery in Passion

It was going to be a long night.

~

It had been a long night for Cassie, and climbing from her bed a little past six the next morning, she'd managed no more than three hours sleep. The storm had been a noisy one, the likes of which she had never heard before. There had been a few times when it had rattled her windows that she thought it would take her house down. But the storm had passed, and she had managed to doze off.

Feeling sluggish, Cassie stumbled from her room, the sunlight burning her tired eyes as she headed to the washroom. She slipped into the shower, sighing at the warm water that pulsated over her aching muscles. Lathering up her hair, Cassie let it sit while she scrubbed her body with soap. It felt great to be under the warm spray, so Cassie lingered in the shower a few moments longer than usual. But when the chill rippled in the air, she shut the water off and pushed back the curtain.

She shivered with the sudden coldness in the room.

Slipping into her robe, she wrapped a towel around her hair and turned to the mirror.

And froze, watching the words, *HELP US*, as it was scrawled in the mist in the mirror.

Without hesitation, she yanked the door open, screaming the whole time she ran down the stairs.

And rammed right into Thomas.

"What? What's wrong?"

She felt his hands on her arms, felt her own heart pounding, and looking up, she was never so glad to see a person as she was him now. "Someone was writing on the mirror."

"What?"

"Upstairs. I got out of the shower, and when I looked at the mirror, someone was writing the words, 'help us', in the mist."

He released her and headed up the stairs, Cassie

followed right behind him.

"There's nothing here."

She looked into the mirror and all she saw was dew. "It was there, and someone was writing it in the mist."

"Cass." He took hold of her arms, a worried look on his face.

"Don't say it." She lifted her hand to stop him. "I know what you're thinking. *She's crazy*. But I'm not. I know what I saw. Weird things are happening here, and I think the place is haunted."

"I thought something was seriously wrong when I heard you scream." He explained while heading down the stairs.

"I know what I saw, Thomas."

"How well did you sleep last night, Cass?"

She stood at the top of the stairs looking down at him while he examined the steps. "Not well, but—"

"Your second night here and a big storm rolls in. Must have kept you awake.

"Well, yes, but—"

"Lack of sleep caused you to see something that wasn't there. I'll try to be quiet down here if you want to catch a nap."

She scowled down at the top of his head. "I don't want to take a nap. I have things to do, and I wasn't hallucinating because of lack of sleep. I may be blonde, but I'm not a flighty airhead that spooks easily, and I don't appreciate the implication."

"I never implied that you were a flighty blonde."

"It was in the tone of your voice."

"You misheard me. Stan, the guy who I called to paint your walls should be here around ten. He'll have a book of colors for you to choose from. As soon as you make your decision, he can get started on the walls, and when he's done, I can get started on the floors."

She huffed at him; he was changing the subject on her, and it pissed her off. "I'll make sure I'm back by then."

"Back?" He lifted his head now. "You're heading out?"

"I have to go to my shop and get things rolling there. What are you doing here this early, anyway?"

"I'm an early riser. I was outside checking my garden when I heard you scream. You didn't lock your door last night."

"Yes I did." She even remembered locking it. It was a habit with her, being from the city.

"Well, it was open when I got here." He walked away and headed to the living room.

Letting out a huff, Cassie twisted, saw the bedroom door to her left was open and decided from now on she was going to keep it closed.

~

First thing on her schedule was getting the utilities hooked up at her shop. And she needed a telephone. Strolling into town hall, Cassie smiled at the gentleman that held the door for her. "Thank you very much."

"My pleasure."

The place was empty, except for the two women standing behind the customer services desks. "Good morning." With a smile on her face, Cassie strolled to the woman on her right.

"Good morning. How can I help you today?"

She was a bright looking woman, possibly in her later thirties, Cassie deduced. She had bright blonde hair wrapped in a bun at the top of her head. Her face was a milky white and her brown eyes unpainted. The sunny yellow suit she wore was nearly blinding.

"I just moved here. I bought the shop next door, and I need to hook up some utilities and phone service."

"Alright. Let's get started." The woman pulled out her computer and typed in her request. "Let's start with your name."

"Cassandra Evans."

She typed it in. "Place of residence?"

"432 Garrison Road." You could have heard a pin drop, that was how silent the room became. "Problem?"

"No, no problem."

"I know it's haunted." She blurted out, hoping that was why the woman had looked at her with such an odd expression when she'd given her address.

"I need you to fill out this paperwork, and we can get started."

Taking the form, Cassie glanced at it and spoke. "I was told that people were murdered in the house and that some say it's haunted. Is that true?"

"I'm not at liberty to say." The woman busied herself on the computer.

"Why not?"

"This is my job and gossip has no place here. Now, if you would fill out this information sheet, we can get the ball rolling."

Frowning, Cassie took the pen and began filling out the questionnaire. "Could you at least tell me who it was that was killed in my house?"

"If you wish to look back into the records, you will have to fill out another form and pay a fee."

What the hell was the big deal? All she wanted to know was who had died in her house. "Will those records tell me who died there as well?"

"For that you'll have to go to the Royal Canadian Mounted Police depot. It's right down the block. I'll get this into the system and be right with you."

It was beyond her why she had to go through all the formality just to find out who had died in her house. It was a small town for pity's sake; small towns were famous for gossiping.

"Here we go. Everything is set up and will be connected first thing tomorrow morning. Is there anything else I can do for you, Miss Evans?"

Yeah, tell me who died in my house and how. "Not at

this time..." Cassie glanced down at the name plate on the desk that read *Betty Talbot*, "Betty." She left the office wondering why the last name sounded so familiar.

Chapter 8

Her belly was rumbling, but her first thought was to kick off her heels and sit back with a nice cold glass of chardonnay. That was if the local bar actually had chardonnay, which they hadn't. Instead, she'd had to make do with a twenty-four pack of beer. It was a poor substitute, but she would have to make due.

Pulling into her garage, Cassie slid from the car and hoisted the bag of groceries she's picked up, then grabbed the case of beer. She had to shift the bag in order to open the garage door, but she managed. Trudging across the lawn, her heels sinking into the damp ground, she lost her balance when her ankle twisted over and nearly lost the bag of groceries. When she tried to pull her foot—and her shoe—out of the muddy lawn, it refused to give.

"Oh, give me a break." Cassie gave it a good hard yank, her foot slid free, leaving her shoe behind, and in doing so, she lost her balance and fell flat on her ass with a squishy thud. "Crap." And to top it off, the bag ripped in her arms and everything inside came tumbling out. "Damn it!"

"Got a problem?"

Cassie looked up, the sun nearly blinding her, but she managed to see the grin on Thomas' face. "I hate this day."

"Having a rough one?"

She took the hand he held out to her, and when he yanked her to her feet, Cassie collided with his chest. "It was, until now," she purred seductively.

"You drink beer?" he asked, releasing her to step back.

"A gorgeous woman, more than ready to be taken, all but throws herself at you, and all you can think about is beer."

"I like beer," he commented lightly, gathering the contents that had been in the bag before it broke.

Discovery in Passion

"You like beer." Cassie snorted, trying to yank her shoe from the ground. The thought hit her hard and had her head snapping up to him. "You like beer; you'd rather have beer than me. Now I get it. You're gay."

"I am not gay." He piled the frozen dinners on top of each other and carefully placed them on the case of beer.

"That explains everything."

"I'm not gay," he repeated, grabbing the bags of chips. "Do you eat anything besides junk?"

Cassie ignored him and continued working on her shoe which was thoroughly jammed into the mud. "You know, you could have simply told me you swung the other way, and I would have understood. I actually have several gay friends."

"I'm not gay," he insisted, angling his face to her.

"Really, it's okay—" She fell flat on her butt when the shoe finally gave with a slippery pop. "I really do hate this day."

Grinning, Thomas set the bags down and held out his hand. "You really are having a rough one."

She took his hand, pursing her lips as he lifted her to her feet. "And then some."

"Tell me about it." He began gathering the bags once more.

"Well, to start with, I didn't sleep worth a damn. The thing this morning freaked me out, and when I go to hook up power at town hall, the woman there refuses to tell me anything about the people that were murdered here. Then I go to the bar and simply ask for a bottle of chardonnay and the bartender snickered at me. 'We don't serve fancy wine here.' I wanted to pop him in the mouth. It's not that fancy, for Christ's sake." She grunted while she picked up the few remaining items left on the damp grass.

"So you settled for beer?"

She shrugged. "It goes down nice on a hot day. Are you seeing anyone?"

"I'm not gay, Cass." He lifted the case of beer with

the frozen meals and chips on top like it weighed no more than a feather and walked to the house.

"Sure you're not. It's always the good looking ones. What a shame." Cassie sighed, watching his tight round ass move as he took the steps up to her deck. She could imagine herself taking a good hold of those cheeks and giving them a firm squeeze. She nearly bumped into him when he stopped short, to set the case on the top step.

"I'm not gay," he repeated, taking her by the arms, hoisting her up and took her lips in a sharp and very potent kiss.

Cassie felt her feet hit the step, felt her head spin and, opening her eyes, saw him looking down at her with a sober expression on his face. "Well, you certainly can kiss. Lucky men."

He threw his arms in the air, before grabbing the case of beer. "You know, just because I like beer and I'm not giving into your advances doesn't make me gay."

Cassie gave an undignified snort. "Right. Oh, hi." The tall thin gentleman who stood in her dining room startled her.

"This is Stan. Stan, Cassie Evans," Thomas introduced, setting the beer and frozen dinners on the counter.

"Pleasure to meet you, ma'am."

"Do I look old? Ma'am, please. Call me Cassie."

"Cassie it is." Stan tipped his head. "I hear you're looking to repaint?"

"You betcha. I hear you have a book of colors?"

"That I do. I'll go grab it, and we can have a look see."

Half an hour later, she had her colors picked out and was more than eager to see them on her walls. "When can you have the colors ready and start painting?"

"First thing tomorrow morning. I'll run to the city and get the colors mixed today. I can be here bright and early tomorrow morning. That work for you?"

Discovery in Passion

"Sounds perfect." Cassie saw Stan to the door, and when she turned back, she saw the stain on the floorboards in the center of the living room.

"It'll be covered up when I install the hardwood." Thomas supplied, standing in the doorway, nearly filling it.

"Someone died there." Her eyes lifted to meet his. "And no one will tell me anything about it."

"Why is it so important for you to find out who it was?"

"Wouldn't you want to know who died in your home?"

"Not really." Thomas supplied with a shrug.

"Well, I do, especially because of that and because of the weird things that keep happening here, and don't look at me like that. I don't care if you believe me or not; I know what I saw; I know what I feel. This place is haunted."

"What proof do you have that anyone actually died here?"

"Pete said—"

"You're taking the word of someone who might have been pulling your chain because you're new to the town. He's put the thoughts in your head, without proper sleep, without proper nourishment—"

"What do you mean by that?"

"That junk you call food. You're not eating properly, not sleeping properly, and you're in a new place, a new town and the word of a perfect stranger has your mind working on overtime. Step back from everything, Cass, and think about it, really think about it."

Frowning, she pulled her hair back, releasing it with a huff, "I'm not normally this jittery, but I've never been on my own before." And the more she thought about it, the sillier it seemed. "Okay, maybe you're right, and now I feel like a complete idiot."

"What you need is a decent meal. This crap you call

food is far from that. I've got some thick steaks in my freezer waiting to be grilled."

"Are you inviting me to dinner, Thomas Healy?" she asked with a seductive grin.

"Dinner, only dinner."

"Right, because you're gay."

"Damn it, woman, I am not gay."

"Prove it?" she teased, moving just a skosh closer to him.

"I already have, several times."

She ran a hand along his firm muscular chest. "I think I need a bit more convincing."

His hand clutched onto her wrist before she could slide her hand any further. "I'm not falling for your game, Cass. Do you want dinner or not?"

"Yes, Thomas, I do." And so much more. But she could wait.

"Great. How does six sound?"

"Perfect. I'll be there with bells on." she teased, her voice low and sexy.

"I'd prefer you wore something more than bells."

She smiled wickedly, saying, "Don't worry; I'll have clothes on."

~

It had been over a year since he had picked up a brush, a pencil or anything to create with. There'd been nothing that had inspired him enough to want to paint. Now, as Thomas stood before the painting he was creating of Cassie, he felt the creative juices flowing.

She had an abundance of beauty, and that alone was incentive enough to want to paint her, but there was something more. Nearly from the moment he'd first laid eyes on her, he'd felt it. She did something to him, woke something in him he'd thought long dead.

Lifting the brush, he dabbed the bristles into the paint he'd hand blended to match her skin tone and began to paint her. Her skin had a golden luster to it and he imagined she sunbathed often in that tiny excuse of a bikini. She had flawless skin that felt like silk. The faint tan lines told him she tanned in both the nude and in the bikini. And he hadn't seen any indication that she'd had any breast augmentation surgery, so that told him they were real. God had been generous with that woman.

Thomas' brush strokes were smooth as he created the goddess before him. When the telephone rang, he scooped it up without thought and answered, "Hello."

"Hey, pal, what's shaking?"

"Same old stuff. You?" He spoke while the phone rested on his shoulder and the paint brush dabbed on the canvas. He'd known Vic most of his life and felt a brotherly kind of love for him. There'd even been a time when Thomas had thought to follow his friend and join the police force. But painting had been Thomas' love. He'd given up his idea of being a cop and lived vicariously through Vic.

"Nothing much. Are you tired of small town life yet?"

Vic asked that exact question every time they spoke, and the response Thomas gave was always the same. "Nope"

"That's a shame. I thought I could introduce you to this hotty I met at the bar last week. She was stacked, pal, and oh so ripe for the picking."

"Your type, not mine." But after saying it, Thomas looked at the painting of the voluptuous blonde that lived next door.

"Come on, man, when are you going to stop dating those lifeless corpses you call women? Christ, remember Margie—did she actually have tits?"

"Vic," he warned.

"Seriously. She was as dull as a broken light bulb."

"Was there a reason you called, Victor?"

"I wanted to say hi."

"You said it; now stop bugging me; I'm working."

"Yeah, on what?"

Thomas laid the brush down and stepped back from his work. "A portrait."

"You're painting?" Vic's voice rang with surprise.

"Yeah."

"No shit?"

"No shit." Thomas smiled, resting his brush in the glass jar of solvent.

"Well, hell, that calls for a celebration. I'm going to go have a beer for you, pal, and let you get back to work. Talk to you later."

Replacing the phone, Thomas took a good hard look at his work. Vic was right; it did call for a celebration. And who better to celebrate it with than the very woman he was painting.

Chapter 9

Thomas was going to swallow his tongue when he saw her. Standing before her mirror, Cassie admired herself in the long flowing red dress with its thin straps, low cut bodice and sweeping back. If this didn't encourage him to make a move on her, he really was gay.

And now for the final touch. Lifting the stick of Seductively Red lipstick, she ran it over her lips, giving them a smack as she replaced the tube on her dresser. That should do the trick.

Heels clicking on the bare steps, Cassie made her way down the stairs. She was going to enjoy making Thomas Healy sweat, and when he was panting and begging her to let him have her, Cassie was going to make him beg just a bit more.

Grabbing her keys, she headed for the back door. Hearing something that sounded a great deal like a whispering voice, Cassie paused. Turning cautiously, she saw absolutely nothing.

"Well, duh, you dummy." Shaking her head, Cassie pulled open the back door, making sure to lock it on her way out.

"Look out, big boy, because here I come." Having learnt her lesson the first time, Cassie took the path around the house rather than having her heels sink into the muddy ground, and headed for the front door of his house. Taking a deep breath, she rang the doorbell and waited.

When the door opened, she had the satisfaction of watching his eyes widen as he caught sight of her. *Oh, yeah, take a long hard look, big guy, and eat your heart out.* "Am I early?"

"No, right on time. Come in." Thomas stepped aside to allow her inside.

Purposely adding sultriness to her walk, Cassie moved past him with a sly smile. "I don't think I've mentioned how much I like your house."

"Thank you."

She shifted, the slit in her dress parting as she moved. "Do you like what I'm wearing?"

"It's very lovely."

You're drooling. "And look, just like I promised." Cassie slid her left leg out, the dress parting nearly to her hip, revealing a garter of bells. She gave her leg a shake, making the bells jingle. "Bells."

He hadn't swallowed his tongue, but she at least had him speechless.

"Gay men don't ogle women's legs."

Thomas blinked, lifted his head and began to walk to the kitchen. "I told you, I'm not gay."

"Probably not, but you are stupid."

"Why, because I'm not falling at your feet, begging to have you?"

Cassie followed him through the dining room to the kitchen which was a good size larger than hers. "For pretending you don't find me attractive."

"I never said I didn't find you attractive. I said I don't date the people I work for."

She watched while he grabbed the steaks already marinating on a plate from the fridge "Do you know how stupid that sounds?"

"To you maybe, but I like to play it smart." He slipped past her with the tray and headed out to the back deck.

Cassie followed.

"After you're done working on my house, would you consider—"

"No." He laid the steaks on the grill, and the juices dripped onto the coils, creating a sharp sizzling noise.

Cassie brow curled in a frown. "Why not?"

Thomas shifted his body towards her and spoke firmly. "You're not my type."

"Really?" She was every man's type.

"Really."

"Okay, fine, what is your type?"

"How do you like your steak?"

"You're evading the question."

"Damn straight I am. My mother raised a smart man. Steak?"

Cassie smiled, feeling incredibly at ease with him. "Well done."

He shook his head. "Ruining a good peace of meat. You don't know what you're missing."

"Neither do you." She countered and took a seat in the soft plush patio chair. "You never did tell me why you moved here?"

"I like the quiet."

"Come on, big guy, share." Crossing her legs, the skirt parting to reveal her bare leg and the bells, Cassie waited for a response. When all he did was walk away without a word, she huffed. The instant he returned, she prodded on. "Why won't you tell me? What's the big deal?"

"I believe this wine will be to your liking." Thomas placed the wine glasses on the table, then lifted hers and filled it with chardonnay.

"Where did you get this?" She was definitely pleased with his choice in wines.

"I have a wine cellar. Whenever I go into the city, I pick up a few bottles of wine." He poured himself a glass.

"You drink wine? I picture you as more of a beer guy."

"I like both, but I'd more likely sit down to a cold beer than a glass of wine. I keep it for special occasions."

"And you have many of those?" Cassie sampled the wine and found it perfect.

"Not so many these days."

"Then, what's the special occasion today?"

"I painted your portrait."

She nearly jumped out of her chair. "Can I see it?"

"It's not completely finished. When it's done, you'll see it."

She sat back down, nearly deflated. "How long will that take?"

Thomas shrugged, and went back to the steaks. "A few days."

She didn't want to wait that long. "So we're celebrating you nearly finishing my portrait."

"We're celebrating my painting."

She snorted. "Seems like a silly thing to celebrate when you were born to paint."

"I haven't painted in over four years."

"Painter's block?"

"My mother died."

She didn't quite know what to say to that aside from, "I'm sorry."

He sauntered to the table, lifting his wine. "Regina had a facility that could possibly help her. She had ovarian cancer, and her doctors in Mississauga couldn't help her. So I flew her to Regina. By the time I got her there, it was too late. They did what they could to make her comfortable but couldn't prolong her life."

"Oh, Thomas, I am truly sorry."

He focused on the steaks. "She wanted to go somewhere quiet, somewhere no one would know us, no one would know she was ill. I grabbed a real estate agent, and we found this place."

"How long did you live here before she died?"

"A little better than three years. She fooled the doctors by hanging on two years longer than they'd predicted. But the last year was bad. She suffered. I did my best, but…" He left it hanging, flipping the steaks.

"Any siblings?"

"No."

"And your father?"

"Never knew him. He died before I was born."

"It was only you and your mother, then? That must

have been incredibly hard for you."

"It was. I was busy taking care of her that I didn't have time to paint, and after...well...I didn't have a reason to."

"Until now." Cassie smiled when her eyes met his. "I'm glad I helped you overcome your painter's block. I knew I had an effect on you."

"I'm not giving in, Cass," Thomas informed her as he took the steaks off the grill.

"We'll see; we'll just see."

~

Cassie had a wonderful time with Thomas, enjoying a scrumptious meal and friendly conversation. And true to his word, he hadn't given in to her. But she wasn't giving up on him yet. She rarely gave up when she wanted something or someone, and though she didn't quite understand it, he mattered a great deal to her.

Entering her house, Cassie regretted not having left any lights on. Clicking the back entrance way light on, it partially lit the dining room but not the rest of the house. Which meant she was either going to have to brave it and go upstairs in the dark or turn a light on like a chicken.

She was braver than that, and, slipping from her high heels, walked towards the stairs. She wasn't brave enough, however, to look towards the living room and quickly scurried up the stairs. Seeing the bedroom door open to her left, Cassie frowned. She was sure she had closed it.

Cautiously, her breath still, Cassie reached out for the doorknob to close the door. A loud bang cracked through the silence in the air, and she jumped back, hitting the door, making it swing all the way open. Her eyes went wide staring into the darkened room lit only by the street lamp outside. There, crouched over a desk was a man. The back of his head was gone, ripped open and coated in blood—blood that was splattered on the wall beside him, and the desk he laid on.

When he turned his head with eyes coated a deathly milky white, she bolted, screaming as she ran from the house. She didn't stop until she got to Thomas' door. Cassie pounded on his back door, rapidly, until she saw the inside door open.

She nearly sent him stumbling back as she lunged towards him, wrapping her arms around his big firm waist.

Her entire body shook.

"What the—"

"He's in the house, and there's blood and...and...oh, God, so much blood."

"What are you talking about? Cass, Jesus, you're shaking like a leaf."

"I went to close the bedroom door—I hate having it open, and I saw him, lying over the desk. His head—oh, God, his head was gone."

"Cass," Thomas took hold of her by the arms and held her out. "You're not making any sense. Now, take a deep breath, and tell me what happened."

She inhaled, but it did little to calm her down. "There was a guy... in the bedroom."

"In your house?"

"Yes." She blew it out, exasperated.

Releasing her, Thomas opened his back door and headed out.

"Wait up." Cassie caught up to him as he headed to her place. "What are you going to do?"

"Check it out."

She followed him through her back door and past her dining room to the stairs. "You're not going to see anything."

He took the steps to the upper floor by twos. "Why is that?"

"Because he won't be there anymore." And heading to the bedroom Cassie saw she was right. "I know what I saw, Thomas."

"Did you have any lights on up here when you saw it?"

"Only the hallway light that's on now, but—"

"Shadows."

"It was not a shadow. I know what I saw, and I'm going to prove that this house is haunted." The lights went off, making her scream.

"Jesus Christ, you've got a set on you. Got a flashlight?"

"No." Grabbing his arm, Cassie clung to him, her legs quivering.

"No? Who in their right mind doesn't think to own a flashlight? Where is the fuse box?"

"The what?" She was too afraid to look anywhere, for fear of what she might see, so Cassie squeezed her eyes tightly shut.

"The fuse—oh, never mind."

"Where are you going?" she asked when he started moving down the stairs.

"Basement."

"What for?"

"Odds are the fuse box is down there. Your nails are cutting into my arm."

"Sorry." She loosened her grip. Clinging to him, Cassie was right there behind him when he took the steps down to her basement. "It's too dark down here. How are you going to be able to see?"

Slipping his hand in his jeans pocket he pulled out a penlight and flicked it on. "Like this."

She was grateful for that tiny sliver of light. "What are you going to do when you get to the fuse box?"

"Check the fuses. You probably blew one, and that's why the power went out."

"Oh, okay." Cassie stopped when he stopped and moved in right behind him. If anything was going to happen, she felt secure in knowing he was big enough to handle it. She was safe as long as she was with him.

"Thought so. Here you go." He flipped the switches.

"It's still dark."

"Do you usually leave lights on everywhere?"

"Well, no..." she sighed, feeling foolish. "How do we know if it worked?"

"We try a light. Know where a switch is down here?"

"I've never been down here."

"You've never—you are a strange one, Cass. Okay, let's go up and see if there's light. Want me to carry you?"

Cassie snarled though she knew damn well he wouldn't be able to make it out in the darkness. That's when a thought hit, and she grinned. "Yes, please."

It was to her utter shock that he actually followed through. When Thomas scooped her up in his arms, Cassie leaned against his chest and was close enough to see the frown on his face. "My, what strong arms you have, Thomas."

He came to a complete stop. "You're playing me." Then dropped her back down on her feet and tromped towards the stairs.

"I wanted to see if you would actually do it." Smiling, Cassie hurried behind him. "You're very gallant. I like that in a man."

"Is there anything you don't like in a man?"

"Sloppiness, rudeness, inconsiderateness, selfishness—"

"Okay, I get the point. You like a perfect man."

Taking the last stepped up, Cassie was glad to see the dining room light on. "No such thing as a perfect man. If that ever happens again, can I call you to fix it?"

"You know how I did it; you can fix it yourself."

"Where are you going?" She asked when he headed to the door.

"Home, to bed."

"Can I come with you?" She hurried after him.

Thomas stopped, and she nearly rammed right into

him. "Cass—"

"I don't want to stay here alone," Cassie pleaded. It took a great deal for her to admit just how scared she was. She didn't like showing her vulnerable side.

He let out a long breath, shoved his hands in his pockets, and nodded. "Fine, you can have the spare room."

"Great! Why would my fuses do that thing to knock out my lights?"

"They're old. It happens with old houses. What did the inspector say about the wiring in the house?" Thomas asked, pushing through the back door.

"Inspector?"

Resting his arm on the rail at the bottom of her deck, Thomas frowned. "You did have the house inspected before you bought it?"

"Of course! I may be blonde, but I'm not stupid. He said everything was up to code. I didn't talk to him; he sent me a fax with his findings."

Thomas shook his head as he opened his back door. "Are you always this impulsive?"

"Yes."

He shook his head again. "The bed's made." Pushing the bedroom door open, Thomas stood to the side.

"Thanks. I know what I saw, Thomas."

"I might have a t-shirt you could wear, if you like."

"Wear for what?"

"Bed."

The smirk lifted her lips slowly as Cassie looked up at him with a sultry look. "I sleep in the nude." She could actually see him swallowing the vision of her nude.

"Rest well." Shifting, he headed down the hall.

"Want to join me?"

"Good night, Cass."

"Good night, Thomas." Grinning, she closed the door, then slid the zipper at the back of her dress down. Stepping out of her dress, she slipped beneath the covers and curled up in the cool cotton sheets.

Closing her eyes, Cassie saw the corpse with his head blown open and sat up in bed, her eyes wide open.

It was going to be another long night.

Chapter 10

It had been a rough night for Thomas. He had spent a great deal of it imagining the naked woman in a bedroom separated from him by one, thin, wall. He knew what she looked like naked, and it played havoc with his dreams all through the night.

He hadn't had a wet dream since his youth. He was thirty-two years old, for Christ's sake. Thirty-two-year-old men didn't have wet dreams, yet he had. Then again, he hadn't had the real deal in quite some time either.

The woman was going to drive him to the brink.

Rising at dawn, Thomas took a long shower, to rid his body and mind of the dreams, then headed out to do some gardening.

Why shouldn't he go for it? Would it be terrible if he did decide to sleep with her? So what if he was working for her. He'd be done working on her place by the end of the week. If he did decide to have a—fling—he didn't have flings. He'd never taken a woman for his own pleasure, only to cast her aside without ever seeing her again. That wasn't his nature. His friend Vic, maybe, but not him.

Besides, if things didn't work out between them, they would be forever reminded of it, living next door to each other. It couldn't work.

"What are you doing?"

He flinched; the trowel in his hand skimmed over the dirt he'd been working. Letting out a breath, Thomas looked up at her.

Jesus, she was a beauty. Her skin glowed, her eyes were blue like the sky above, and her smile put the brightness of the sun to shame. He was momentarily speechless.

"Cat got your tongue?"

"Gardening," he said quickly, continuing what he was doing. *Stop thinking of her.* Yet his mind refused to oblige.

"Like vegetables and stuff."

"Like vegetables and stuff." He smiled "There are bagels in the bread box on the counter, or I can make you something if you want more than a bagel."

"I'm not much of a morning person. I'll eat later." When she knelt down beside him, Thomas nearly lost all thought when the dress parted to reveal her bare leg. "My grandmother used to garden, but in the later years, the arthritis in her hands got to be too much. I always loved stealing vegetables from her garden, but it wasn't much fun when I found out she knew I was stealing them."

She loved to chatter, and he found he rather liked the sound of her voice. "Did you sleep well?"

"I did, thank you. Um, I guess I should head back to my place." She stood, let out a long sigh and waited.

Closing his eyes, Thomas dusted his hands, before standing to dust his knees. "Want me to check things out for you?"

"That would be lovely. You're such a dear."

And she definitely knew how to play him. He was becoming a sucker for that soft innocent voice she used on him when she needed something. Thomas said nothing, taking the path by his garden and to the back alley to her place.

"Did you sleep well, Thomas?"

And there was that seductive voice that went right through him to grab hold of his loins. "I always sleep well," he lied.

"I heard you get up around five this morning. Do you always get up this early?"

Not that early. "Yes." He pushed her back door open, shaking his head. "You really need to learn to lock up."

"I was a little scatter brained last night."

He headed straight for the bedroom and still saw nothing. "Place looks clear."

"Are you going to be here today, working?"

"No, Stan's going to be here painting."

"Oh, right. Well..."

She was close enough to him that he could smell the faint aroma of the perfume she'd worn the night before, and it sunk right into him. *One quick fling, Thomas; step out of your comfort zone, and go for it.* "Catch you later." *Coward.*

He hurried from the house and out into the beating heat of the sun. What he needed was to focus on his garden and not on taking Cassie to his bed and ravaging her scrumptious looking body.

But as he sat down in the dirt, even the round plump vegetables reminded him of her.

He was doomed.

~

Cassie left Stan to do his thing with painting her walls and headed to the police office. What she needed were answers, and she was determined to get them. She pushed through the front doors with her shoulders squared and her chin firm.

It was an ordinary looking office, which surprised her a great deal. Not that she had ever been in a police station before, but from what she'd seen on TV, this simple office looked nothing like a police station. In the center of the room was one long counter desk; behind it sat a woman with graying hair wrapped in a tight swirl at the top of her head, busily tapping away at a typewriter that looked like it might be as old as the woman herself. To the left of the desk were two doors, both closed, and a long hallway.

With a bright smile, Cassie approached the woman. "Hello—" She was cut short when the woman raised her hand to silence her. Cassie huffed and waited.

When the woman finally stopped clicking on the ancient keys she looked up with a bright smile. "Sorry about that; I lose track easily. Now, what can I do for you?"

"I was wondering if I could speak to the man in charge."

"Staff Sergeant Hopkins is on the phone at the moment. May I ask what it is you need to see him about?"

The woman seemed personable enough, so Cassie relaxed. "I was hoping he could help me. I recently moved into a house on Garrison Road, and I was told that three people died in that house. I'd like to find out a little more information about that, if I could."

"Give me one second. You can have a seat in the waiting area while I call the sergeant."

The waiting area consisted of five shabby, steel-framed chairs with very little stuffing left in the faded blue seats. Smoothing her skirt, Cassie took a seat and waited. The walls in the office were in a dull brown but it was the photos of the Mounties on their horses that caught her attention. She'd always found a man in uniform to be sexy, and there were plenty of sexy men in the photos covering the dull brown walls.

"Miss? The sergeant will see you now."

Cassie stood, gave her skirt a tug, before walking in the direction the woman pointed to. She entered the office and saw the officer sitting behind a shabby looking wooden desk cluttered with papers. When he stood, Cassie admired the blue shirt and blue trousers normally worn by officers but thought how he was the exception. He was not handsome in his uniform like many officers were.

His graying hair was slicked back from a bony face that was severely wrinkled with age. And when he held his hand out to her, the smile on his face only made him look even more homely.

"Good day, Miss—I'm sorry, I didn't get your name."

"Cassie Evans." She took the hand and felt the firmness of his grip.

"Please, have a seat, Miss Evans, and tell me what it is I can do for you."

Discovery in Passion

At least the chair in this office was more comfortable than the ones in the waiting area. She took a seat, crossing her ankles as she spoke. "I live at 432 Garrison Road, and I was told three people died in my home ten years ago. Is that true?"

He cleared his throat, leaning back in his chair. "Yes."

"Who?" When he hesitated Cassie pursued. "Please, I only want to know who it was that died in my home, to put my mind at rest."

"Edward, Luanne and Eddie Talbot."

"Can you give me some information on what happened?"

"I can give you a brief run down. Eddie Talbot shot both parents before shooting himself in his bedroom."

Her stomach clenched. "Which bedroom?"

"First room to the left, at the top of the stairs."

Her heart started to pound. "Did he shoot himself in the head?"

"Why are you so interested in this, Miss Evans?"

"Because I live in the house where three people died."

"It was ten years ago."

It didn't matter. "Shouldn't I have been informed when I bought the house that people had been killed in it?"

"You'll have to discuss that with your real estate agent."

She most definitely would. "Why did he kill them?"

"No one knows; killed himself without leaving a note. If that's all, Miss Evans, I have a busy day and—"

"Are there any surviving relatives that I could talk to?"

"Let it go, Miss Evans." He stood, moved to the door and held it open. "Have a nice day now."

Pursing her lips, Cassie stood and moved to the door. "Did you know the Talbots?"

"Have a nice day, Miss Evans."

Annoyed, Cassie left the office, vowing to find out more information. What was the big deal? Why couldn't he tell her?

Climbing into her car, she headed back home.

Chapter 11

Cassie could smell the paint the instant she entered the back door. Though it was strong, it was a refreshing smell. It meant the house was becoming hers.

Even if it was haunted.

Hearing the chatter of several male voices, Cassie peeked into the living room and saw not only Stan, busy painting, but three other men, all dressed in army green overalls with paint splattered on the fabric. But it was the lovely aqua marine walls that really drew her attention.

"Wow, that looks great."

All four men turned to her voice and two of the men gaped as they looked at her.

"It's a little darker on the walls than it was in the can. I was worried you might not like it," Stan said, wiping his sweaty brow.

"Oh, I really like it. You guys are fast."

"This is only the first coat." Stan supplied. "It'll get another before we leave. We'll start on the kitchen and dining room tomorrow, while Tom starts on the hardwood."

"Wonderful. This is really starting to shape up. Can I get you boys anything to drink? It's hotter than hell today, and I'm sure you're all working up a sweat in those coveralls."

"We're fine, Cassie, thanks anyway."

"Alright, then I'll get out of your way. If you need me, I'll be outside." She left them to finish up, happy with the outcome so far, and headed over to see her favorite neighbor.

Only the screen door was closed. When she knocked and didn't receive an answer, Cassie opened it and stepped inside. "Hello?"

She heard the soft sounds of music playing and followed it to a bedroom down the hall and to her left. The door was open, and she could see Thomas' back as he stood in front of what she thought was a painter's easel. Easing through the door, she moved to his left and saw what he was busy doing.

It was her nude portrait.

"Wow."

His hand paused, then slowly he angled his head to face her.

"That's incredible. It—I look so real."

"I didn't hear you knock." He placed his brush in the jar with the cleaning solution, then put his pallet of paints on the table beside him.

"I did; you didn't answer, so I thought I'd see where you were. This is truly incredible Thomas. You are a genius."

"No, I'm not." He moved to the table he had set up for his paints, and lifting the cloth, he wiped the paint from his hands.

"Very few people can paint something this lifelike. You rank right up there with Van Gogh and Picasso. It's no wonder your work is in such high demand." It amazed her how someone could create anything as lifelike and beautiful as Thomas had on the canvas. Everything from her skin tone to the blue in her eyes looked incredibly real. As if her own eyes were watching her.

"Was there something you wanted from me?"

"Now that is a loaded question." When he didn't turn to face, her she sighed. "My place smells like paint, so I thought I'd come by and see what you had planned for the day. But I see you're busy working. I'll let you get back to it."

"I'm finished for now. I was about to make myself some lunch. Care to join me?"

"How sweet of you to ask. Yes, I would love that." She batted her lashes, but that, too, went unnoticed. Cassie followed him to the kitchen, wondering what it would take for him to give in to her. "Can I have it when you're done?"

Discovery in Passion

"No."

Her brow furrowed. "Why not?"

He pulled out a large glass bowl, before heading to the fridge. "I want to put it on display at one of the art galleries I have my work showcased at."

Cassie watched Thomas pull fresh vegetables from the fridge then began cutting them up. "I think not."

He tilted his head to her but continued to chop up vegetables. "Why not?"

"I will not have a bunch of strangers ogling my naked body. No way, no how." Feeling warm, she slipped from her blazer and hung it over the back of the wooden chair in his kitchenette. There was no way she would consent to letting him display her portrait.

Laying his knife down, Thomas looked at her with surprise on his face. "You wear practically nothing half the time. I don't see why it would be such a big deal."

"The fact is I am wearing nothing in that painting. Nothing." She repeated stronger. "And I don't dress *that* skimpily."

"You call what you're wearing today not skimpy?"

Cassie looked down at the short black skirt that came to her mid-thigh with the slit on the left side and the silk camisole blouse in blue. Sure, the camisole was silky and revealing, but she'd kept her jacket on in public. "What's wrong with what I'm wearing?"

"It's very revealing."

"It's hot outside. I wanted to be comfortable."

"Then what's the big deal about me hanging your portrait up."

"I'm naked! Okay, yes, I wear revealing clothing, but all the major parts are covered."

"All the major parts are covered in the portrait."

"Fine, you can't see my nipples or bush, but you can see everything else."

"Your arm is covering your breasts, just like the blouse is covering them now. Same thing."

"No, it isn't. And you can't display it without my consent, which I am not giving. End of conversation. What are you making?" Cassie asked, ending the conversation—she hoped—as she moved in beside him.

"Salmon salad." Lifting the knife, Thomas continued chopping up vegetables.

"Never had it before. Can I help?"

"You can grab the salmon from the fridge." After a short pause, he added, "What am I supposed to do with your portrait, then?"

She could hear the annoyance in his voice. "I'll buy it from you, if you tell me how much."

"It's the first piece of work I've done in four years that is worth displaying, and you won't let me display it," Thomas grumbled.

"Suck it up, big guy. I'm sure you'll paint something else just as fabulous." She yanked on the plastic lid, trying to pry it open. "How do you open this container?" When it suddenly gave, splashing salmon all over her shirt, Cassie fumed. "Great."

"All you needed to do was push on the center and the side would have popped. Here." He handed her a dishcloth, taking the container of salmon from her and placed it on the counter.

"Well, you could have mentioned that before." Huffing, she began wiping at the liquid and the salmon. "Perfect, now I smell like salmon."

"It'll wash out."

Her eyes lifted, and Cassie saw where his were focused. Smack dab on her breasts. She smiled slyly. "Oh, I'm sure it will, but in the mean time, I should get as much out as possible. Look at this; it's all over the place." Cassie grinned to herself watching his tongue slip out between his watering lips. "I need to use a damp cloth." Moving to the sink, Cassie ran some water over the cloth, but when she turned back she saw his arms crossed over his wide chest and a frown on his face. "What?"

"I know what you're doing."

"Cleaning myself," she said innocently.

"Like hell. Damn it." Grabbing hold of her by the arms, he yanked her up and took her mouth in a hard, possessive kiss.

Smiling inwardly, Cassie wrapped her arms around his neck as he bent at the waist and let his glorious mouth seduce hers.

And what a mouth it was. His lips were soft, firm and full, and damn if he didn't know how to kiss. She felt herself being lifted off the floor and wasn't entirely sure if it was her imagination or reality.

When he started moving, Cassie knew it wasn't her imagination. Opening her eyes she saw he was heading down the hallway and obviously to his bedroom. Her pulse shot through the roof, and she felt as if she might explode with anticipation.

"This is a mistake," he panted, planting her on her feet.

"The hell it is." She wanted to feel his hair, but the band he had it tied back with got in her way. With a quick tug, Cassie pulled it free. When it spilled out over his shoulders, it nearly took her breath away. He was magnificent. "Oh, baby."

Her breath came out in a gasp as he yanked her against his chest and captured her mouth with his. She threaded her fingers through all that glorious hair while his hands slid over her back, down to her buttocks and back up. As he slid the zipper on her skirt down, she felt herself moisten.

It pooled to the floor, and she made busy work undoing his jeans zipper and button, eager to see that hard bulge she felt pressing against her abdomen.

Her body quivered for him.

Taking her hands in his, he moved her back towards the bed, his mouth busy on hers. When she bumped into the bed, she sat back, allowing him to press her down onto it. His hands slid beneath her blouse and made dozens of goose-bumps form on her skin. As he skimmed over her breasts to lift the blouse over her head, she panted, arching, wanting. And then, finally, his mouth dove down capturing her breast. Cassie gasped, her body aching for more.

He suckled. He devoured. He aroused.

His fingers skimmed over her belly, sliding her silk panties down. She wiggled, helping him to remove them and couldn't wait for the release. Cassie moaned a protest when his mouth slid from her breast, but then he dove down between her legs, lapping up her juices. The heat shot straight into her belly and Cassie spread her legs to allow him easier access.

He was a clever man and knew exactly where to touch to make her come. She felt her climax tighten in her belly right before it exploded in a near earth shaking orgasm.

"God, yes, yes, yes," Cassie panted, her fingers digging into his silky hair as he took her over the edge.

When he rose up and braced himself over her, his golden brown hair fell over his shoulders, framing his gorgeously strong face, Cassie thought she might just have fallen in love.

"Take me," she murmured lazily.

He removed his jeans, ripped the shirt over his head, and as he lowered down over her, pressing himself into her, Cassie felt the pressure building deep inside.

She wanted, and she was going to take.

Bowing her back, she welcomed him inside and reveled in the pressure he caused as he plunged deep. With each thrust she could feel it building, and when he lowered his head to suckle on her breast, Cassie let herself go.

"Oh...my...God..."

Before her orgasm had a chance to subside, he lifted her up and off the bed, spinning her around. She was confused for a moment, but then he pressed her against the wall, and plunged. Wrapping her legs around his waist Cassie rode the glorious wave of sensations he induced inside of her.

"Yes," she cried out as he pumped her ruthlessly. She felt insane with need, devilishly crazy to have more. Her fingers threaded through his hair; she yanked his mouth to hers and shoved her tongue between his lips.

He spun her once more, pressing her down onto the bed again, lifting her knees higher, he plunged even deeper. She arched her back as he pumped her over and over.

"Now, yes, now!"

Cassie felt him pulsate inside of her, creating a ripple effect driving her to another orgasm. As he grunted with his release, she felt her body level out. "Oh, wow," she laughed, panting as he finished.

Thomas collapsed beside her, and when she shifted her head, she got a full view of his entire body. "Sweet God, you have muscles everywhere." And one particular muscle was still as hard as a rock.

"I work out," he managed, panting.

"I'd say. That was quite a work out *we* just had." Giggling, Cassie rolled onto her side and toyed with the fine hairs covering his chest. "I've never had this many orgasms at one time before. Sure, it's been months since I've been with a man, but damn…" She laughed, kissed his chest, then snuggled against his arm. "You're definitely not gay."

"Told you."

Laughing, Cassie nuzzled closer, gladly willing to stay this way for a good long time.

When the phone rang, she sighed. "Let it go." He didn't move, and that pleased her immensely. But when someone knocked on his door several moments later, she knew he wouldn't ignore it.

"I'd better see who that is."

"Mind if I stay here. I don't think I can walk."

Thomas laughed as he sat up, grabbing his jeans and shimmying into them.

What an ass that man had on him. Even that was muscular. And she didn't mind watching it as he exited the room. Sighing contently, Cassie rolled onto her back and smiled. That had been one hell of a nooner.

"Door's for you."

"What?" she responded lazily, looking up at Thomas. She hadn't even heard him re-enter the room.

"Stan, he needs you back at your place."

She sat up with deep regret. "Why?"

"Didn't ask. Told him you were in the washroom."

Cassie smirked, caught the skirt he tossed at her. "You lied."

"Yeah. I think this is yours, too."

She caught her underwear, still grinning. "Why didn't you tell him we were having sex?" Cassie slipped into her clothing, regretfully.

"It's none of his business."

"Uh huh." Was he modest? "Is the invitation for lunch still open?"

"Of course." Thomas scooped his hair back, then slipped an elastic band around it, making her sigh.

"I like your hair down." Moving to him, she trailed a fingernail along his chest.

"It gets in the way."

"Ever had something you just couldn't get enough of, Thomas?"

"Sure."

"I think you might be that for me. See you in a bit." Grabbing her shoes, Cassie sauntered from his house, feeling pretty damn good.

Chapter 12

Thomas felt pretty damn good and didn't have one ounce of regret. They'd had sex, wonderfully fulfilling sex. Cassie wasn't his usual type, but she was so much better. The fact that she had spoken of her other lovers right after had been the only downfall.

He continued chopping the vegetables for the salad, and while he added the salmon, his mind wandered to what had started the whole ball rolling. The woman was a flirt, loved to tease, and she knew precisely what to say and do to make his body ache. And all it had taken for him to give in was to see her wiping her soiled shirt. Okay, it had been his imagination as she'd been wiping her shirt that had finally pushed him to take her. He was only a man, after all, and seeing a woman as well endowed as Cassie caressing her own breasts was something fantasies were made of.

Now that he'd had her once, there was no way he was letting her go.

The shouting from next door caught his attention. Wiping his hands, he stepped outside, hearing Cassie calling out to Stan. He hopped the short white picket fence separating their properties just as Stan and his men came rushing out the back door of Cassie's house.

"What's up?"

"Fucking place is haunted. Jesus, I thought the rumors were bullshit, but, man, I saw it." Stan exclaimed.

"I'm not paying you if you don't finish the job," Cassie called out from the back door, her hands on her hips, a furious look on her face.

"Keep your money, lady."

"Damn it!"

Baffled to what was going on, Thomas headed to the door and confronted Cassie. "Problem?"

"I thought men were supposed to be tough? Damn chickens won't stay in the house because it's spooked.

And they left the job half done. What the hell am I supposed to do now?"

Spooked. How could grown men be such idiots? He could understand it coming from a woman, but the men should know better than to believe rumors. Shaking his head, Thomas moved past her and into the house.

"Know anyone else who could finish the job?" Cassie asked, following him.

"Yeah." Thomas scratched his head, wondering if he was going to regret this, and decided he had no other choice.

"Who?"

"Me."

"I thought you said you didn't paint houses?"

"Normally, I don't, but I'll make an exception this time. Ever painted before?" Thomas asked, giving his attention to Cassie. He caught a good look at her now and couldn't help the grin that slipped out.

"What's so funny?"

"Have you looked in a mirror lately?"

Her brow wrinkled. "No. Why?"

"You're hair is a mess, and your make-up's smudged." And she looked absolutely radiant.

"What? Damn it." Cassie rushed to the washroom, then screeched. "Why didn't you tell me before I left your place?"

"I didn't notice it." But it was lighter in her house. "You sure it wasn't you that scared them off?" he teased.

Cassie came down the stairs with a scowl on her face. "You're funny. Jerk." Pursing her lips, she sat on the bottom stair. "Now what?"

"We paint."

"We?"

Picking up a roller, Thomas held it out to her. "We."

"I don't have a clue how to use that thing."

"You strike me as a fast learner. I suggest you change into some grubby clothes first."

Discovery in Passion

With a frown on her lips that he found absolutely adorable, Cassie spun around and trudged up the stairs.

Heading to the living room, Thomas was grateful that Stan had at least managed the first coat. It wasn't going to take them long at all.

An hour later, with the temperature a balmy thirty-two degrees centigrade in the house, the walls were done in the living room.

Cassie dropped her brush into the paint pail and dusted her hands. "I'm starved and dryer than a bone. Want a beer?"

Wiping his forearm across his forehead, Thomas nodded. "I'd love one. We never did get around to eating the salad I made. I could go get it, and we could take a break and finish it off."

"Take a break?" Cassie whined.

Thomas laughed. "I thought, while we were on a roll, we might as well start on the kitchen and dining room."

"I changed my mind. I don't want it painted. White is good; I like white."

He caught the beer she threw at him and pressed it against his forehead first. "What's the matter, Cass, not used to a little manual labor?"

"Hell yeah. That's why I hired people to do it for me. Besides, it's too damn hot." Cassie popped the top on her can of beer and gulped down nearly half. She was absolutely beautiful. Her hair was tied up in a flirty ponytail at the back of her head that was now damp and clinging to her neck. Her face was shimmering with perspiration, as was her chest right above the black cotton tank top she wore. Thomas thought she was the most beautiful woman he had ever seen.

"Thomas?"

"What?" He shook his thoughts clear.

"I asked if you wanted me to throw a sandwich together for us. What were you thinking about?"

"A sandwich would be fine." He could save the salad

for later.

"You didn't answer my other question," Cassie stated, coming up beside him, a purr in her voice that went right to his loins.

"I was thinking how the colors you chose are perfect for you. Vibrant," he lied.

"Uh huh, and I'm supposed to believe that because you think I'm a blonde airhead. Try again, big guy."

The simple motion of her nail along his arm sent shock waves of lust rippling through him. "I thought you were starved?"

"I am, but it can wait. Why are you so secretive?"

"Because I know how it irritates you." He stroked the damp strand of golden silk from her face and felt something ping inside of his heart. "You're so beautiful."

"I'm sure. I probably look like crap right now and no doubt smell worse. I'll get those sandwiches made." She reached up to kiss him, and he knew he had just fallen in love.

~

It was a little past three in the afternoon, and the sun was beating down hard. Sitting on her deck with the patio umbrella shading them, Cassie and Thomas gobbled down the sandwiches they'd put together. Her arms were aching something awful, and her back was sore from painting, but she felt oddly refreshed. Maybe it was the food and beer, but she'd lay odds that it had more to do with the glorious sex she'd had only hours before.

Seeing Thomas stretched out in his chair directly across from her with his shirt off, wearing only faded blue jeans with the top button undone, reduced her body to mush. Cassie wondered if she could convince Thomas to join her in a nice cold shower for some raunchy sex.

"It wouldn't take us long."

"Huh? What?" She shook her head clear.

"To paint the kitchen and dining room."

"That involves hours of work. I have something better

in mind." She slipped from her chair and boldly sat down on his lap and began toying with his damp hair. "Something less sweaty."

He captured her hand in his, slowly nibbling on her knuckles. "Is that all you ever think about?"

"Baby, looking at you like this, with your shirt off and all those bulging muscles gleaming with sweat, makes me think of nothing else." Cassie stood, spreading her legs over his as she straddled him. "I'm helpless to my needs."

"It's the middle of the afternoon, Cass, and we're outside."

Yet as she moved against him, slowly gyrating, she could feel him harden. "It sure is."

"I'm not having sex with you where anyone could see us."

"That's half the attraction. It's dangerous," she murmured against his ear, slipping her tongue out to slide it over his earlobe.

"You're incorrigible." But even as he said it, he hoisted her up and carried her into the house while she giggled against his ear.

When he sat her on the bed and ripped off her shirt, Cassie pulled away before he could go any further. "This time it's my turn." Quickly, she drew the zipper down on his jeans and released his penis from the restraint that had held it back.

Cassie nudged him down onto the bed, then spread his legs and knelt between them. With her eyes on his, she took him all the way into her mouth.

She was sure she saw his eyes cross.

"Jesus, your mouth is hot."

Smiling, Cassie continued sliding her tongue up and down the shaft, stroking him with her hand. When his head fell back and he moaned, she knew he was close to his climax. Shimmying out of her shorts, Cassie released her hold on his dick, then straddled him.

"Sweet God," Thomas gasped as she lowered down, taking him all the way in.

Her body was on fire, and Cassie felt like a wild woman as she began bucking over him. His hands came up to squeeze her breasts, and she felt it tingle right into her belly. Throwing her head back, she pumped him furiously, feeling the climax building ever so slowly, gloriously slowly. And when he pulled her down to take her lips in a ravenous kiss, she felt herself explode. Then he gripped her hips, bent her legs and began pounding her good and hard. Cassie thought for sure her eyes would cross.

He erupted inside of her with a hot burst that sent her over the edge.

"I must have died and gone to heaven," Cassie panted after finally catching her breath. "This is way too good to be true." She screeched when he pinched her butt. "What was that for?"

"Just reassuring you that you are still alive."

"I know I'm alive, you dummy. It was a figure of speech." She sat up, giving his hair a tug. "I don't want to move."

"We have painting to do," he reminded her.

She fell back over him, pouting. "Can't move, legs broken."

He laughed, kissing the top of her head. "Then I'll paint, and you can catch a nap."

She nuzzled into his chest. "I'd rather you didn't move either. I like this spot; it's rather comfy." She closed her eyes and drifted off to sleep.

Chapter 13

Thomas regretted leaving her alone in her bed, but Cassie had been so completely out of it that he figured he could get started on the kitchen and dining room, then surprise her with dinner in bed. And maybe a little roll in the sack after.

She was insatiable with her lust, and it was rubbing off on him. He'd never been one to indulge in mid-day sex or crave sex the way he craved it when he was with her. But Cassie was doing something to him, and he really didn't mind it.

Whistling quietly, Thomas taped off the ceiling, counter and cupboards. It was only five in the afternoon, which gave him plenty of time to get the first coat on and bring her dinner in bed. He'd hurried back to his place after leaving Cassie asleep in her bed and had put together a quick casserole which was now simmering in his slow cooker. It would be done and ready in an hour, plenty of time for him to get a full coat of paint on the walls.

He wasn't fond of the pale salmon color she'd chosen for her kitchen and dining room, but he wasn't the one living with it. It was a good thing the walls were white and recently painted, or he might have had to put a coat of primer on before painting them.

The house was dreadfully hot. Cassie really needed to get someone in here to hook up central air before she cooked in the heat. Wiping his brow with the back of his hand, Thomas continued taping off the areas he didn't want touched by paint.

The faint female voice he heard disappointed him. He'd hoped Cassie would stay in bed until he was finished. Angling his head, fully expecting to see her coming down the stairs, Thomas frowned when he saw no one.

Shrugging it off, he went back to his work.

She'd lived in this house for less than a week, and it

was already shaping up pretty decently. The woman definitely knew how to get what she wanted and get it now. She'd managed to get him, hadn't she? Even when he'd vowed to himself he would never give in to her. Here he was, feeling the after-glow of glorious sex and painting her walls, hoping she wouldn't wake before he was done so he could surprise her in bed.

He felt something brush against his arm and, shifting, thought he saw movement behind him. Seeing nothing, Thomas brushed it off as possibly hallucinating from the heat, and went back to his work.

He stopped, thinking he heard someone weeping. It was quiet, which made him think it might be Cassie. Laying the roll of painter's tape on the counter, Thomas moved to the stairs. The sudden, loud bang made him jump. He ran up the stairs, just as Cassie flew out of her room, stark naked.

"Did you do that?" they asked simultaneously.

"No." Again, it was said together.

"What was it then?" Thomas inquired.

Cassie curled her arms over her body and responded, "I've heard that sound before. I thought it was a car backfiring."

"Wasn't a car," Thomas stated, heading up the stairs. "It came from up here."

"Damn, is it cold in here? Do you have fans going?" She shivered.

"You're naked sweetie." He moved to her, wrapping his arms around her and felt the chill on her skin. "Let's find you something to wear." Hooking his arm over hers, he led her to her room.

"Did it sound like a gunshot to you?"

What an odd thing for her to ask. Yet he thought she was right. "You've heard a lot of guns going off?" He grabbed the robe hanging on the back of her door and remembered it from the time she'd answered the door wearing nothing but.

"No, well, just in movies. It kind of sounded like that. What were you doing when it happened?"

Thomas wrapped the robe around her as she slid her arms into the sleeves. "Prepping to paint downstairs."

Angling her head to the clock, Cassie frowned. "How long have I been asleep?"

"About an hour. If you're still tired, you could go back to bed, and I'll finish up downstairs. I made a casserole, and I was thinking we could share it in bed."

Her blue eyes twinkled with amusement. "You did, huh?"

He tucked a strand of hair behind her ear, kissing the top of her head. She smelled like apple blossoms. "Unless you'd rather help me paint downstairs?"

"No, I rather like your plan. How long before I can expect you and the casserole in my bed?" she asked with a huge dollop of seduction.

"An hour."

"Plenty of time for me to have a bubble bath." She ran her fingers along his arm before kissing him. "Want to join me?"

"You're a tease, Cassie." And he loved it. "Enjoy your bath." He left her to finish his work.

~

"You don't know what you'll be missing," she called out to him, sauntering to the washroom, pausing at the bedroom to the left. She felt something eerie coming out of the room, something she couldn't really explain and decided she was never opening that door again. Closing the washroom door, she sat on the edge of the tub and ran the water. She scouted through her many bottles of bath crystals and oils, then decided to simply go for the lavender bath bubbles and added two caps full.

Dropping her robe, Cassie dipped her toes into the water first before stepping into the frothy warm water. Sinking beneath the bubbles, she leaned back and let the warm water cascade over her skin.

She felt absolutely wonderful. If she were to look into a mirror, Cassie was sure she would be glowing. Shutting the taps off, she pulled the shower curtain closed, then shut her eyes and relaxed in the tub.

There was a sudden chill in the air, so she slid further down under the warm water.

She could easily live off of hot sex, warm baths and the occasional meal for as long as she lived. She'd had lovers in her lifetime, and she'd enjoyed most of them—there had been the odd few who had done nothing for her—but she couldn't ever remember feeling this glorious afterwards. Thomas Healy definitely had something special that her body reacted to.

And thinking of him and what he did to her body was making her want him all over again. They'd gone two rounds, and she was eagerly waiting for the third. They'd have a nice little meal of whatever it was he said he'd made, then she'd jump him and ride him until they were both too exhausted to even think.

Opening her eyes, she reached out for her bath sponge and saw the shadowed form of a man through the shower curtain. "Changed your mind, did you, big guy? Well, what are you waiting for, there's plenty of room for two." But when she moved the shower curtain aside, she saw no one.

Baffled, Cassie closed it again and shrugged off the feeling. Using the sponge, she began to wash her body, lathering her skin up with bath oils she knew would drive Thomas crazy when he smelt it on her. Good, she wanted to drive him crazy. Guess she hadn't done what she'd promised herself by making him beg for her. Oh, well, she'd finally managed to seduce him to bed; it didn't matter now that she'd once been miffed at him for rejecting her.

The chill rippled over her skin. Lifting up to run a little more warm water, Cassie saw the shadow once again. She yanked the shower curtain back only to see no one. That's when it struck her. It hadn't been Thomas that had come into the room because, if he had, she would have heard the door or his footsteps. She'd heard neither. That only meant one thing. Pulling the plug, she stepped out of the bathtub. Grabbing a towel, Cassie wrapped it around her damp body, the chill now gone but not the fear.

"Thomas," Cassie called out, opening the washroom door and stepped out.

She froze as she gazed upon the door across from her, slightly ajar. She was damn sure she'd closed it.

There had been a presence in the washroom with her, but it hadn't been Thomas. Seeing the bedroom door open now, she knew without a doubt who it had to have been.

Cassie backed up, bumping into someone and let out an ear splitting scream.

"Whoa. It's only me."

She spun around, not sure if she was glad to see Thomas or not. She slapped his chest good and hard, making him wince. "Why didn't you answer me when I called you?"

"I just got into the house. The casserole's done, so I thought I'd come up and let you know. What's wrong?"

She'd been here, done this before, and she wasn't about to let him mock her for her jitteriness again. "Nothing," she lied, deciding the best thing to do was put it out of her mind, and she knew one thing that would manage to do that. "I wanted to let you know I finished my bath." She headed to her bedroom and let the towel drop to the floor. "Anytime you're ready, I'll be waiting." Angling her head over her shoulder, she gave him a smoldering grin. "In bed."

~

As promised, Cassie was waiting in her bed, completely naked, when Thomas had brought the plates of casserole and wine to her room. She had been ruthless, insisting he join her naked in bed while they ate. He'd finally given in and shed his jeans and shirt.

She didn't feel the slightest bit shy about her nudity and him seeing it. He had, after all, painted her completely naked. And they'd had sex twice already, so she didn't bother tucking the blanket under her arms, covering her breasts, as she sat up cross legged and ate.

"I went to see the police about the murders that happened here."

"Oh," he said simply, lifting his fork to his mouth.

"The sergeant wasn't overly helpful."

"What was it you wanted to know?"

"Details. Why did the son kill his parents? How were they killed? How did he kill himself?"

"And what did he tell you?"

Cassie frowned, lifting the glass of wine to her lips, taking a sip before responding. "He shot both his parents, before taking the gun and shooting himself in the bedroom across from the washroom."

"You shouldn't have dug into it, Cass."

She lifted her eyes to his with bafflement. "Why not? I have a right to know what happened in my house."

"Some things are better off not known."

"I don't agree with you." Cassie set her wine down on the bedside table.

"Since you found out someone died in your home, you've been jittery and seeing things."

"What I've been seeing aren't hallucinations," she insisted.

"You're letting your imagination get the best of you."

"I am not. Why is it no one sticks around in this place for long? Why haven't the past few owners stayed? Maybe they saw things too."

"Or the house wasn't to their liking. Think rationally, Cass. Did you see anything before you found out someone had been killed here?"

"Well, no, but—"

"Case closed."

Discovery in Passion

"What about Stan and his men? They saw something that spooked them enough to leave without finishing the job."

"If what Pete said is true, everyone in this town has heard the rumors. I'm sure Stan and his guys have heard it to. The mind is very suggestible. That's all it is, Cass, an over active imagination"

She pursed her lips and decided there was no point arguing when he wasn't willing to budge an inch. What she needed was more information. And the first place she was going to look was with the previous owners.

Chapter 14

The real estate office was small and not only dealt with the purchase of housing in Passion, but two of the small towns near by, as well as rental properties. Cassie took a seat in the waiting area as instructed by the perky redhead behind the information desk. She leafed through a *Vogue* magazine half-heartedly while she thought about what she was going to ask Steven. Cassie decided it was best to just get to the point.

When Steven popped out of his office and called her in, Cassie was determined to get the answers and was not leaving until she did.

"Sorry for not booking an appointment, but I appreciate you fitting me into your day." Taking a seat, she smoothed out her skirt.

"I had a lull; you couldn't have timed it better. How are things at the house?"

"Funny you should ask. I want to know who lived there before me, and I want names and numbers."

Steven tilted his head with a baffled look on his face. "May I ask why?"

"I want to know why they decided not to stick around."

"Is there a problem with the house?"

"Yes. It's haunted." She waited for the burst of laughter. When all he did was clear his throat and look down at his hands, Cassie knew he knew. "Why didn't you tell me when I bought it?"

"It was only rumors, people getting skittish in a new house. I had no proof," he supplied.

"You could have at least told me people had been killed in it before I bought it."

"Would you still have bought it?"

She pursed her lips. "No, I suppose not."

"All I am legally liable to tell you is that the house is for sale and help you with the purchase. The house is legally sound, no major defaults, therefore I saw no reason to divulge its past."

Cassie huffed and thought maybe she might contact her lawyer. "What reason did the previous owners give for leaving?"

"Cassie—

"Just come clean with me, damn it. You owe me that much at least."

He folded his hands on his desk. "They claimed they heard someone crying, claimed the spot on the rug kept coming back no matter how many times they cleaned it."

"What else?"

He huffed. "They claimed they saw things."

"Like what?"

"If you want to put it back on the market, Cassie, I can take care of that."

"I don't want to sell it. It's my home now. All I want is some answers. What did they see?"

"A dead body in the left bedroom at the top of the stairs."

She closed her eyes and let out a long breath. "I've never been one to believe in the paranormal. I thought it was all hooey." She opened her eyes and met his squarely. "But now I know it's not. I'm living in a haunted house."

"Cassie—"

"Know any exorcists or someone to take care of them for me? Never mind, I'll take care of it." She stood and smoothed out her skirt. "Would you be able to get me any information on the deaths?"

"No, I'm afraid not."

"Didn't think so. Do you know if there are any relatives of the late Talbots in town?"

"Calvin and Betty Talbot."

Betty, the woman who she'd spoken to about hooking up her utilities. Now she understood why the name had sounded familiar. Talbot. "How is she related?"

"Calvin, her husband, was the nephew and cousin of the deceased Talbots."

"Thank you, Steven."

"Cassie." She pausing as she reached the door. "Don't stir things up that might be better left alone."

She didn't want to stir things up; she only wanted answers, and as Cassie walked into town hall, she was determined to get them. "Hi there, remember me?" Her voice was perky but cut with a slight edge. She was tired of getting the runaround.

"You were in here the other day."

"Right on the nose. So, your last name is Talbot. I happen to be living in your husband's relatives' house. Maybe you remember it. The one on Garrison Road?" Cassie understood now why the woman had gone white when she'd heard where Cassie was living.

"I know where you live," she spoke quietly, her eyes darting around.

Cassie saw the woman at the end of the desk busy trying to pretend she wasn't listening. "Is there somewhere we could go to talk?"

"I'm working, Miss Evans, and I can't just up and leave."

"I know that. Maybe we could arrange a time to meet for coffee, or you could come by my place—"

"No!" Cassie was startled by the quick response. "Please, just go." She hurried away, and Cassie stood staring, wondering what it was she was in such a hurry to get away from.

"What are you doing?"

Cassie shifted her body and smiled up at Thomas. "Hello, handsome. Are you looking for me?"

"I came to pay my bills." He took her by the arm and drew her to the side. "What are you doing?"

"Asking some questions." Why did he look so annoyed?

"Did it ever occur to you that talking about their

deceased relatives is a touchy subject?"

Frowning, Cassie looked back to where Betty had been standing. "No, I didn't think about that."

"It was only ten years ago. It could still be a sore spot for them."

She of all people should know that, having recently lost her grandfather. "I wasn't thinking."

"Do you have the keys to your shop?"

"Yes, why?"

"We can go talk in private."

She walked out with him and let them into her shop. "If you're going to yell at me—"

"I never yell."

"Fine, get angry at me—"

"I said we could talk. What makes you think I'm angry at you?"

"You look angry."

He stared at her for a moment, before lifting her to her and planting a kiss over her sulky mouth. "Better?"

"I like kissing you." She smiled, wrapping her arms around his waist. He was several inches taller than her which made it harder to wrap her arms around his neck.

"Why are you so obsessed with finding out about the people that died in your home?"

"They died violently in my home." She released him reluctantly.

"In the past."

"They died in *my* home,"

"Okay, I get that. But can't you just let it go?"

"No." She paced the empty room. "I know you don't believe what I see is real, but I know it is. Those people, mainly the son, still linger in that house, and I can't live there knowing they died violently."

"Then move out."

With a tilt of her head and a frown on her face, Cassie retorted, "Why does everyone want me to move out ? It's my home. Mine."

"What do you propose?"

"I don't know. It scares the hell out of me, and that bedroom gives me the major creeps, but I refuse to leave. It's the first thing I have ever owned on my own. If I give up, give in and move out...well, my grandfather would be right."

"I'm lost."

Letting out a long breath, Cassie leaned against the wall and began. "I've been content breezing along with my life, doing whatever I pleased, which was pretty much shopping, lounging and socializing. I've never had a real job and my parents gave me money to live. When my grandfather died, he left a special clause in his will in regards to me. He would leave me the inheritance, but I would not receive it until I did something lucrative with it. Specifically, start a business, buy my own place and learn to live on my own."

"So you decided to come here and start fresh."

Her face brightened. "Yes, exactly."

"If you give up and sell the house, you'd lose the money?"

"No, it's more than the money. He would be disappointed in me."

"Your grandfather?"

"Yes."

"Who's dead?"

"Yes."

He scratched is chin. "How can he be disappointed in you then?"

She huffed. "Okay, I know you probably think it's foolish, but I feel that he would be disappointed in me if I gave up."

"I don't think it's foolish. I felt the same way after my mother died. Would she be disappointed in me because I couldn't paint?"

"You were really close with your mother weren't you?"

"It was always only the two of us. She worked her ass off trying to give me a good life, and when I finally could help take care of her, I made sure she had everything she needed. I loved her dearly."

He really was a softy at heart. To look at the guy, with his tall frame, his wide shoulders and muscular features, you wouldn't think he was soft. But inside he was a cuddly bear. And she wondered what he would say if she told him that was how she thought of him. Walking to him, she wrapped her arms around his waist, and craned her neck to look up at him. "She'd be very proud of you, Thomas."

"And your grandfather would be proud of you, too." He kissed the top of her head, and she absolutely melted.

"I hope so."

"Look, if it means this much to you, I know a guy."

"A guy?" she teased, running her nail along his chest.

"He works for the RCMP in Mississauga. He might be able to help you out."

"Really. That would be wonderful."

"Stop it."

"Stop what?" Cassie batted her lashes innocently.

"Trying to seduce me."

"Make me." He pinned her arms behind her back making her giggle.

"What are your plans for this place?"

"I don't need my hands to seduce you, Thomas." She had other more devious ways.

"I have no doubt, but this is much safer for me. What are you doing with this place, Cass?"

"Trinkets, remember?" She rubbed her leg up against his, narrowing her eyes in a seductive glance.

"How do you plan on displaying them?"

"In cabinets and shelves. I know I'm getting to you, Thomas."

He released her and moved to the door. "I have bills to pay."

"I'll be waiting for you at my place. Don't be long."

When he left, shaking his head, Cassie burst into laughter. Lord, she was having fun with him.

Chapter 15

Cassie enjoyed teasing and tormenting Thomas every chance she got, and though she'd only known him for a few weeks now, she was getting to know him pretty well. She knew he liked quiet time and often found him sitting alone in his living room with music playing faintly in the background. And she knew that he loved to cook, and if he hadn't chosen art as his passion, he would have been successful as a chef.

He rarely raised his voice, but when he was angry, you knew it simply by the way his voice dipped lower and his words slowed. It wasn't often that he was angry; mostly he was soft-spoken and quite sweet. He doted on her any chance he got.

Even though Thomas worked long, hard hours repairing her house, he always had enough energy for her and often chose to give her backrubs or massage her feet. And, now he even volunteered to build shelves and cabinets for her trinkets. He truly was a dream.

While Thomas worked on her house, Cassie devoted her time to getting her shop up and running. It scared the hell out of her. What did she know about running a business? Sure, she'd taken a short course on how to start a business, but the thought of running one, owning one, maintaining one, still scared the hell out of her. But she was going to make it work one way or another, for her grandfather and for herself.

She'd placed an ad in the local paper and posted signs at the grocery store and town hall. To her surprise, she'd had three girls call her, interested in applying for a job in her shop. After interviewing them, Cassie decided two of them would work out nicely. One of the girls—Jaycee—was just out of high school and eager to start working full-time. The other—Belinda or Bell, as she preferred—was in grade ten and looking for something part-time.

She'd hired them both and asked that they start immediately. There was quite a bit of work needed to get everything up and ready before opening, and both girls had jumped at the chance to start work immediately.

Now all she had to do was set up a payroll account.

Entering the local bank, Cassie hoped they'd be able to accommodate her. She stepped up to the customer services desk with a bright smile.

"Good afternoon. How may I help you?" the woman behind the counter asked.

"I would like to see someone about starting up a payroll account."

"Do you have an account with us already?"

"Yes, I do. I had my funds transferred a month ago. Cassandra Evans." She pulled out her bank book and ID and slid it over the counter to the woman dressed in a horrible orange jumper, with dark black hair that looked like she'd dyed it the day before.

"If you'll take a seat in the waiting area, I'll have one of our loans officers informed of your request."

"Thank you." Awfully formal, Cassie thought, heading towards the chairs. She didn't even have a moment to take a seat when her name was called.

"If you'll come with me, Mr. Talbot will help you with what you need."

"Talbot?"

"He's our bank manager and also one of the loans officers. Here you go." She stepped aside, allowing Cassie to enter the office.

"Good afternoon, Miss Evans. Please, come in and have a seat."

Cassie glanced at the name plate on the desk as she took a seat, then back up at the man before her. *Calvin Talbot*. His hair was thinning at the forehead but still a deep vibrant brown. His face looked as if he might be approaching his forties, but she was never a good judge on age. He was tall, stocky and wore a trim fitting brown suit. "Any relation to Edward and Eddie Talbot?" She had to make sure.

His face dropped but he held his hand out to her firmly. "They were my uncle and cousin. How did you know them?"

"I didn't. I'm living in their old house. Have you lived here long?" She couldn't believe her luck. Here was a direct descendant of the ghosts that were invading her home, and she could finally get some answers.

"All my life. Now, I'm told you want to start a business account?" Calvin pulled out his computer.

"Yes. I'm starting a business here in town. You might have heard about it. *Cassie's Collectables* on Main Street."

"Sorry, no. I'll show you a list of the accounts we offer, and we can go over which would best suit your need, and decide from there."

"Sounds great. Were you close with your uncle and cousin?"

"Of course. Now, here we have—"

"What was Eddie like?"

His face lifted and his eyes went a shade darker. "Did you come here to open an account or to discuss my deceased family?"

"Both, actually. I had no idea I would find you working here when I came in, but I'm damn glad I did." Cassie smiled brightly, hoping to put him at ease.

It didn't work. "While I'll be happy to help you open your account, I am not obliged to discuss my personal life. If you wish to carry on, we may do so, but only with the account and nothing more."

Well, he'd certainly put her in her place. "I'm just curious why he would have killed his family." Calvin stood, and she quickly changed her mind. "Okay, fine, we'll stick to business." Twenty minutes later, she had her new account and had been rushed from his office with a quick hand shake and a hurried goodbye. It baffled her why he was being brisk with her. She could understand him being jittery when talking about his relatives, but he seemed more annoyed that she would speak of them.

It made her even more curious.

Cassie arrived at her house to find yellow caution tape across her doors. Pursing her lips, she grabbed the doorknob and was in the process of ducking under the tape when Thomas spoke up from his yard.

"Don't you know what yellow caution tape means?"

Cassie swiveled around, shielding the afternoon sun from her eyes with her hand. "Caution."

"Don't enter."

"It says 'caution'. *Approach with caution*, not *don't enter*."

He shook his head. "If it's taped across a doorway it indicates no entry. I just put the final coat of polyurethane on the hardwood. It'll be wet for hours."

"Okay, I'll tiptoe then."

"You can't go in, period. I can't risk you bringing dust or other particles of dirt and lint into the house until it's dry."

"You're kidding me, right?"

"Nope. I packed up a few of your things and brought them to my place. You can stay here until it's dry."

Cassie grinned slyly as she moved towards him where he stood by the adjoining fence. "You packed some of my things, huh? Like what?"

"The basics."

"Underwear?" When he didn't respond and walked away, she ran across her property to his. "What was that, Thomas? I didn't hear your response."

"Because I never gave one."

She caught up to him at his back door, still grinning. "Did you pack my underwear?"

"Yes," he grumbled.

"Oh, so you had to have gone into my underwear drawer to get it. Did you enjoy going through my delicates, Thomas?"

"I didn't really bother to notice."

Cassie moved in front of him before he entered the house. "Then why are you blushing?"

"It's hot outside," he said simply.

"Yeah, uh huh. Not! Wanna try again, big guy?" When he moved around her, she continued after him. "You did notice, and that's why you're blushing. Did you enjoy going through my delicates, Thomas?" she teased ruthlessly.

"I thought we'd barbeque some steaks for dinner."

"You can't avoid me, Thomas." Cassie jumped in front of him, smiling. "Admit that you enjoyed going through my underwear, and I'll let it go."

"No, you won't, because you enjoy tormenting me."

"True, but you're so much fun to torment. You get this glassy eyed look, and your cheeks get all pink. You try your damnedest not to be embarrassed by either turning away or rubbing a hand across your face, but I know better." She stopped him by planting her palm against his chest. "You're embarrassed."

"Okay, fine, I'm embarrassed. Happy?"

"You're cute when you're embarrassed."

"Lord, woman, you're going to be the death of me."

Laughing, Cassie decided to give him a break. "How long until I can get back into my house?"

"Maybe noon tomorrow. I'll have to go check it out to see if it's dry, but your furniture won't be allowed back in for at least another day."

"What? How am I supposed to function without furniture?"

"By staying here until the floor's cured." He headed back to the kitchen; she followed.

"How much did you pack for me?" she asked cautiously.

"Enough to last you a few days."

"Plenty of underwear?" Her voice lifted teasingly.

"Don't start."

Laughing, she jumped up onto his back and nuzzled his ear. "Oh, baby, I've only just begun."

~

Later, as Cassie lay curled up beside him, her head resting on his chest, enjoying the afterglow of love making, she couldn't help but push her luck just a bit farther. "I couldn't help but notice you chose mostly my red delicates. How did you come to that decision?"

"Go to sleep, Cass."

She smiled but prodded on. "You would have had to go through the drawer to see the red ones, which tells me you pawed a great many of my delicates. Did you hold each one up, imagining me in them and deciding if you would pack them for me?"

"I'm trying to sleep here."

Not giving up, Cassie rolled on top of him making sure he had to look at her when she spoke. "Did you hold them against your face, imagine ripping them off of me?" She squealed when he threw her onto her back and pinned her to the bed. "Oh, yes, baby, be forceful with me."

"Oh, I have something a lot more devious planned for you, my dear."

"Oh, yeah, what might that be?" Her voice shifted seductively.

"This."

She burst into laughter as he tickled her mercilessly.

Chapter 16

Since she wasn't allowed in her house, Cassie decided it was the best time to get things prepped for her shop. What she needed was to do inventory and categorize everything she had to determine what to would charge for each item.

She'd called both Jaycee and Belinda to ask if they would be available to help and was delighted when both said yes. While Thomas worked on the shelving units, Cassie and her two employees categorized her inventory.

Three hours into it, Cassie was feeling cross-eyed and a little overwhelmed. She decided it was break time for everyone and, despite Thomas' protests, made him sit and have a drink while they took a break.

With no chairs available, they sat on the bare tiled floor, enjoying their bottles of pop.

"Can I ask you a question, Cassie?" Bell inquired, opening her bottle of pop.

"Shoot." Her feet had begun aching an hour into her day, and she'd decided it might be best if she found a pair of comfortable flats to wear instead of heels.

"Did you really buy the spook house?"

"The what?"

"Spook house. The old Talbot place," Bell clarified.

"Oh. Yeah. You call it the spook house? Mind if I ask why?"

"Don't start, Bell," Jaycee warned.

"People say it's haunted."

"It's only a rumor," Jaycee supplied, sending Bell a nasty glare.

"Lots of people have seen things," Bell justified.

"What have people seen?" She had Cassie's full attention now.

"Things. Spooky things."

"Be more specific." Cassie sat up, curling her legs to the side. Maybe wearing a skirt to work wasn't such a good idea, either.

"People are freaked because Eddie Talbot killed himself and his parents in that house. So they make things up," Jaycee added.

"Percy Adams said he saw something just the other day when he was helping Stan paint."

"Percy Adams is a bonehead whose brain is fried from too much drugs."

"What did he say he saw?" Cassie asked Bell. All Stan and Percy had said was that they wouldn't work in her house as long as the dead walked around the rooms. When she'd pressed them for more information, neither had been willing to give her details.

"Said he saw Eddie walking around upstairs, in the room he killed himself in. Percy went to the washroom and saw Eddie. Scared the living piss out of him."

"That's enough, Bell," Jaycee warned.

"No, it's okay. I want to hear it. I see him, too," Cassie said reassuringly to Bell.

"So the place is haunted?"

"I think it is. Did either of you know anything about what happened that day Eddie killed his family?"

"We were both too young to remember much," Jaycee supplied.

"My mom says Eddie and his dad were always really close. They did everything together. She said that there've always been rumors that someone else killed them and made it look like he did it."

"Eddie was found with the gun," Jaycee stated with a snort.

"That doesn't mean anything."

"Why does your mom think someone else did it?" Cassie inquired, breaking into an argument she was sure was about to happen.

"'Cause Eddie was a good guy, loved his parents, never got into trouble. Why would he suddenly kill his family, then himself?"

"That's what I've been trying to find out. You guys

know Calvin Talbot?"

"Sure, he's the bank manager," Bell supplied before gulping down a fair amount of her Pepsi.

"I tried to talk to him yesterday, but he got upset with me."

"Probably still a sore spot with him," Bell added. "He's the one who found them."

Cassie's eyes went wide. She glanced at Thomas who sat silently across the room. "He found them?" She turned back to Belinda. "How long after they were killed?"

"Right after. He showed up and heard the final gunshot. He had blood all over him from trying to revive his aunt and uncle. Calvin was utterly devastated; he went away for a few months. His in-laws said he and his wife—well, girlfriend, at the time—Betty, went on vacation to grieve."

"I've met his wife. She wasn't very friendly to me."

"Betty keeps to herself mostly," Jaycee said, then finished off her pop. "I'm ready to get back at it." She stood, dusting off her jeans.

"Me, too." Bell stood, carrying her bottle to the trash can by the back door.

"I'll be right with you." Cassie moved to Thomas and waited until the girls had left the room before speaking. "Well, what do you say now, big guy?"

"About what?" Thomas stood, placed his half finished bottle of Pepsi on the floor and went back to is work.

"My house being haunted."

"Hearsay."

"Come on. Even after hearing what Bell said others have said—what Percy said—how can you still be so skeptical?"

"I'm being logical." He put on his safety glasses, then lined up the wood under his saw.

"You're being pigheaded. You need to stay at my place for a few days and then you'll see. What about your friend? Did you call him?"

"I did."

"And…"

"He said he would see what he could find out."

"Good. Maybe you should call him and tell him what Bell said about people thinking someone else did it."

"Maybe I'll wait and see what he finds out first. It might take some time for him to get the information. In the meantime, can you try not to interrogate the locals?"

"Hey, I'm a local here now, too, and I wasn't interrogating anyone." She sulked.

Smirking, he lowered down and kissed her. "You have employees waiting for you."

Still sulking, she walked away, then pausing, swiveled towards him with a bright smile. "I could send them home, and we could—"

"No!"

Her brow lowered. "You don't even know what I was going to say."

"I know where your mind wanders half the time, and the answer is no. We are not having sex in your shop."

Her lips curled in a pout. "Party pooper." She shifted and felt a wave of dizziness wash over her. She shook it off and went back to work.

~

While Cassie took her shower, Thomas slid the stew he'd prepared the day before into the slow cooker. Picking up the telephone, he dialed Vic's number and listened while it rang. When it was finally answered, Thomas noticed the slur in his friend's voice that either meant he'd just woken him from sleep, or he was drunk.

"Rough day?"

"And then some. What's up?" Vic slurred.

Not completely drunk, but he'd had a few. "Not much. Did you get a chance to look into that case I asked about?"

"Haven't had a chance, sorry."

"Not a problem. Something new has come up. Seems

people are thinking someone else did it. It's only hearsay, but I thought I would swing it by you anyway. Vic, you okay?" It was five in the afternoon, and his friend was already drinking. Something wasn't right.

"I'm going through a rough case right now. I'll look into this for you and get back to you by the end of the week. So, how's the sex life going? Still getting it on with the blonde?"

Thomas glanced towards the hall to where Cassie was currently lathering her body with soap. "She's an incredible woman. I've never known a woman like her before. She's beautiful, smart and funny." And if he didn't stop now, he was going to sound like a bubble-headed teenager in love.

Part of it, at least, was true. He was pretty damn sure he was falling in love.

"Ooh, sounds like Tommy-boy is smitten. Can't wait to meet her. Gotta run, pal, catch you later."

"See ya." Replacing the phone, Thomas leaned against the counter, his eyes focused on the hallway that led to the woman he was sure he was falling in love with. He couldn't seem to get enough of her and found the more he was with her, the more he wanted to keep her near him. When they were apart, his heart ached.

Yep, he was falling in love.

A quick glance at the slow cooker told him he had plenty of time. Kicking off his work boots, pulling his sweaty t-shirt over his head, Thomas headed down the hall to join Cassie in the shower.

Entering the washroom, he heard her singing softly to herself and felt his heartbeat quicken. And when he pulled the shower curtain aside, his mouth watered.

"Decided to join me after all, huh?"

Her voice was like liquid honey, and every time she spoke in that low sultry tone, he felt his bones weaken. "Save any hot water for me?"

"Oh, there's plenty of hot water, but you won't be

thinking of the water once you join me."

No, he wouldn't. Slipping from his jeans, he stepped into the shower and took what he wanted. Her mouth was always warm, always eager, and when she kissed, she devastated.

Her body was slick, warm and ready. Her soapy breasts pressed against his chest and he could feel the nipples harden as he held her tight in his arms. And when she grabbed hold of him, Thomas knew this was not going to take long. Spinning her, she braced her hands against the wall while he lifted her hips to accommodate him. The instant he entered her, she wrapped around him, pulling him all the way in, and he knew he was a goner.

With the hot water splashing down onto his back, he pumped her until he felt her quivering around him and then, only then, did he let himself go.

Chapter 17

It took three days before Thomas would allow her back into her house, and still he insisted she not drag her furniture into the house for another day. At least she had her bedroom, and because she was a persistent type of woman, Cassie convinced Thomas to spend a few days at her place. He was insistent that what she saw was only a figment of her imagination, and she was ready to prove him wrong. When nothing out of the ordinary happened the first night, she was discouraged; when nothing happened the second night, she was pissed.

She was not imagining the ghosts.

On the fourth day, they were busy carting in her furniture, with the help of Pete, when Cassie noticed the stain on the hardwood floor. While Pete was grabbing her dining room chairs, Cassie pulled Thomas aside.

"Look."

He looked to where she was pointing and frowned. "What did you spill?"

"I didn't spill anything. That is the spot that was on the carpet, the spot that was on the floor boards, the spot where two people were killed."

He knelt down, placing his hand onto the spot and frowned.

"It wasn't there a few minutes ago, and you know it. But it's pointless discussing it because it'll be gone by tomorrow. It just shows up and disappears. I'll make you a bet that if we go up to the spare bedroom, he'll be there, lying over the desk with the gun at his side and blood dripping onto the floor."

"Cass—"

"Why don't you believe me?"

"You're being irrational."

"This house is haunted by the three people that died here ten years ago."

"Do you have any idea what you sound like?"

"Look at that spot."

"It's a spot. Granted, a huge spot that will take some time and effort to remove, but it's only a spot."

"A blood spot in the exact place where two people were murdered."

"Cass." Thomas sighed.

"No, don't. I am not making this up. I know what I saw, what I see, and I am not losing my mind."

"Sweetie."

"Don't." She pulled away from him, too hurt to let him touch her. "Just finish bringing in my stuff." She marched up the stairs, slammed the washroom door. Sitting down on the toilet, she had a good cry.

She wasn't seeing things; she wasn't losing her mind. Damn him for not believing her.

Grabbing a wad of toilet paper, she blew her nose.

It hurt that he didn't believe her, that he thought she was some flighty blonde with an overactive imagination. She wasn't. She had a brain; she was smart, had excelled in school and even had a high IQ. And she'd never been one to let her imagination get the better of her.

And why the hell was she hiding in the washroom, blubbering her brains out? She wasn't the type to cry over the slightest thing. Big deal, he didn't believe her; that didn't mean she should be sitting in the washroom, crying.

Yet she remained where she was for over half an hour doing just that.

~

Thomas couldn't sleep. Cassie was lying beside him, but she wasn't next to him. He'd hurt her feelings earlier by not believing her. Okay, for practically accusing her of being flighty and irrational. He'd thought it, and he was sure she'd picked up on it. Why else would she have spent a half an hour in the washroom crying? He hated that he'd made her cry.

Damn fool.

Discovery in Passion

Slipping from under the covers, Thomas slid out of bed and pulled on his jeans.

He'd make it up to her by fixing the spot on her floor. One of them must have spilled something without knowing it. How else could you explain the spot? He'd have to work quietly, not wanting to wake her, which meant hand sanding. That was fine, it would be hard, but he deserved it for making Cassie cry.

Grabbing his supplies from his place, Thomas hurried back to Cassie's and prepared to clean and repair the soiled area.

Maybe he would make her breakfast in bed. His rose bush was in full bloom; she'd like it if he cut off a few blooms and placed them on her breakfast tray. Cassie loved roses, and her skin always reminded him of rose petals. Soft and silky.

And if breakfast in bed wasn't enough to tell her how awful he felt, he would do more. A nice elegant dinner in a fancy restaurant. They had never been out on a real date; it was about time he took her on one. She deserved it.

Help us.

Thomas turned to what he thought sounded like a female voice, expecting to see Cassie behind him. Cocking his head to the side, he was baffled that she wasn't behind him.

Shrugging it off, he went back to work sanding the floor by hand.

He nearly jumped out of his skin when the icy cold hand came to rest on his shoulder. Spinning around, he saw no one.

Oh, but he had felt her.

Like a cold shiver, she penetrated him, surrounding him with her presence. He couldn't see her, but he felt her. He knew she was there.

Help us.

"Oh, hell." Rubbing a hand across his face, he tried to

rationalize what he was hearing and feeling. Shaking it off, he returned to his work and stumbled back when he saw two bloody bodies lying on the floor before him.

"Holy fuck." He jumped back.

"Talking to yourself?"

He spun around, his eyes wide and was utterly glad to see Cassie standing at the bottom of the stairs. "Look away." He rushed to her, spinning her away from the gruesome scene. "You shouldn't see that."

"See what?" She tried to look over his shoulder, but he refused to let her. "Thomas, what is going on?"

He looked over his shoulder and was damn glad the bodies had disappeared. And the spot, too. Then he realized how foolish he was being. Had he seen what he thought he'd seen, or was he over-tired and imagining things?

"You're as white as a ghost," she said after he finally released her. "Ghost! You saw a ghost, didn't you?"

Thomas rubbed his chin, staring at the spot where he'd thought he'd seen two dead bodies. He had seen them, hadn't he? And he had felt her, hadn't he?

"What did you see?" Cassie prodded.

"It's crazy."

"I know; trust me, I know. I've tried rationalizing it, but I finally gave up. What did you see, Thomas?"

"I felt someone touch my shoulder. I heard someone, and I thought it was you." He looked back at her. "I felt her—I didn't see anyone, but I felt her. And then I turned, and I saw..." This was nuts.

"What did you see?"

He rubbed his chin a little harder. He was nuts, had to be nuts. Yet... "Two bodies, on the floor, dead."

"You saw them?"

"I...yes, I think so. Jesus, Cass, this can't be real."

"I know, baby, I know." She took him into her arms, and he felt her warmth surround him. "This is bizarre. I see Eddie, and you saw his parents. You have to tell me what you saw."

"No." He shook his head. "It's too gruesome."

"Please! I saw Eddie with half his head missing. I can handle anything."

"It was right on that spot." He glanced at the spot which was now gone.

"I know. I told you."

Turning back to her, Thomas pulled her into his arms and held her tight. "I'm sorry I doubted you. I'm sorry I made you cry." He lifted her chin and kissed her forehead. "Can you forgive me?"

Cassie smiled slyly, and he knew he was in trouble. "I guess you'll have to find some way to make it up to me."

"I already have plans. Why are you up anyway?"

"My stomach felt a little queasy. I woke, and you weren't there, so I came looking for you."

"And you found me." He scooped her up into his arms. "I told you not to eat all that ice cream before bed."

"But it was so good. Want to come back to bed and…rub my tummy?" she said seductively.

She knew exactly what to do to make him turn to mush. "I would love to."

Chapter 18

"What do you mean you won't let me stay here?"

"Just that. You need to pack your things and come live with me." Thomas insisted.

"Live with you? I like my home, and I see no reason why I need to leave it." Yanking the cupboard door open with a bit more force than needed, Cassie grabbed a cup.

"You need to leave because it's not safe for you here."

She spun around and regretted it instantly when the room continued to spin around her for several seconds. Damn that was getting annoying. "How is it not safe?"

"I noticed the roof sagging in some spots."

"What? It is not. You made that up. You just don't want to have to see what you saw last night, and by staying here, you think you'll see it again. You're afraid. Oh, my God, the big guy is actually afraid of something." And wasn't that hilarious.

"I am not afraid."

He was to, and it was the most adorable thing she had ever seen. Here he was, Mr. Tough Guy, with his broad shoulders and bulging muscles, the epitome of tough, and he was afraid of seeing ghosts. It was adorable. "Its okay, baby, I'll protect you from the scary ghosts."

Thomas snarled at her, pulling away to pour himself another cup of coffee. "I don't like you staying here with…that."

"This is too funny." She poured her coffee and, lifting it to her lips, suddenly felt a wave of nausea wash over her.

"You could sell it and easily make a profit."

"I don't want to sell it. It's my home." Cassie set the coffee down on the counter and waited for the nausea to subside.

"You've only had it for two months, and you haven't been in it that much with the renovations and all."

"It's still my home."

"Your grandfather would understand."

Oh, that was dirty. "Maybe he would, but I'm still not selling it. What could possibly happen? Nothing. All they do is show up looking all dead and bloody and—oh."

"What?"

"I don't feel very well." With a hand on her unsettled belly, Cassie made a dash up the stairs for the washroom. Five minutes later, she exited the washroom feeling somewhat better but incredibly weak.

"You okay?"

She looked up to see Thomas leaning against the wall beside the washroom. "I don't know. Was that ice cream bad?"

"I just bought it the day before, but I'll make sure the date isn't past due."

"Great. I think I'll pass on breakfast." Her appetite was suddenly gone, and was it any wonder after spewing her guts in the toilet.

"You should at least try some dry toast."

"Maybe later. I need to get dressed and ready to leave." She moved carefully to her bedroom, worried her stomach might roll over again.

"Leave for where?"

"Work. I have more stuff to do, and it isn't going to get done without me." Bending over to grab some underwear from her drawers wasn't such a good idea. Cassie felt her stomach rise and, straightening out, tried to swallow it.

"You're in no condition to be going anywhere."

"I have to. The girls are expecting me, and I have too much to do." She placed a hand to her belly willing it to settle down.

"I'll go to the shop and help them with whatever needs doing. You…" he pushed her to the bed, "need to rest."

"No, I need the washroom." Darting from the room,

she slammed the washroom door before he could enter. When she finally came back out, she knew he was right. "Okay, I'll stay home today. I'll write out what needs to be done."

"Are you going to be okay here by yourself?"

She smiled, feeling warm all over at his concern. "I'm sure the ghosts will behave while I'm sick."

Thomas frowned at her. "I wasn't worried about the ghosts. I was worried about you being alone while you're sick."

"You are such a sweetie. I'll be fine. This too shall pass. I hope." She lifted to her toes, then decided a kiss might not be the best after vomiting. Cassie hugged him instead.

Cassie wrote out what she wanted done in her absence, then eagerly let Thomas tuck her in bed. If she hadn't felt so utterly crappy, she might have persuaded him to join her.

~

The hour nap she'd taken seemed to do wonders. Waking, Cassie felt fresh and much better. Deciding to go to her shop after all, she took a quick shower. It must have been the ice cream, she deduced, stepping beneath the pulsating shower head. That will teach her to gobble down two bowls full.

It might be a while before she decided to indulge in the creamy delight again.

Placing a dollop of shampoo in her hand, Cassie began to lather up her hair. Thomas had been such a sweetie. The worry in his voice and in his eyes was incredibly touching. He really was a sweet man, even if he was trying to convince her not to stay in her own house.

Of course, she was going to keep it; this was her home and no spirits of the dead were going to take that from her. Stepping beneath the showerhead to rinse her hair, she felt a sudden chill in the air. Reaching out to turn the hot water up, she could have sworn she heard the bathroom door open.

"Thomas?" Pulling back the shower curtain, Cassie froze.

The man standing at the sink had light brown hair that was damp with sweat. He wore a pair of green coveralls and dirty work boots. And he was most definitely not Thomas.

"Get out," she shouted, pulling the shower curtain against her nudity, covering herself up. He didn't even flinch. "I'll scream." The sudden snap of gun fire in the air produced the scream she had threatened. Frightened, Cassie watched as the bathroom door flew open and the man ran from the room.

Grabbing a towel, she wrapped it around her body and cautiously opened the bathroom door to peer outside. Seeing no one, Cassie slipped from the room and saw the bedroom door across the hall wide open.

Her stomach rolled looking at the corpse of Eddie Talbot lying over his desk, his head gushing with blood and brain matter. And when he angled his head and opened his eyes to her, she felt the room sway around her.

~

He was quiet as he entered Cassie's house, not wanting to wake her if she was still asleep. Leaving his boots at the back door, Thomas walked through the dining room, his eyes momentarily darting to the living room, and grateful not to see anything, he hurried up the stairs.

His heart nearly jumped out of his chest when he saw Cassie lying on the floor at the top of the stairs.

"Cass. Oh, Jesus." Falling down beside her, he tested for a pulse first and was damn glad when he felt it. There had been a time, not that long ago when he had found another woman on the floor, only she hadn't had a pulse. His mother had died on the floor of her bedroom, alone.

"Cass. Come on, baby, wake up!" Forgoing trying to revive her on the floor, Thomas whisked her up into his arms and carried her to her bed. Her towel fell away but it was the first time he didn't notice that fantastic figure of hers. "Cassie, come on, baby. Come back to me." When she moaned, it was the sweetest sound he'd ever heard. "That's my girl. There you go, open those baby blues."

"Thomas?" she slurred.

"Yeah, sweetie, it's me. I knew I shouldn't have left you alone." He berated himself as he pulled the covers up over her body.

"I felt better after my nap; well enough that I'd decided to go in to work. But then I..." She sat up and her body swayed. "Oh, wow."

"Just take it easy." Thomas propped some pillows up behind her head. "I'll run down and get you some juice. I won't be long." He kissed her forehead and regretted having to leave her even for the brief amount of time it took to grab the juice. He found her still in the same spot with her eyes closed when he returned. "Cass?"

Her eyes opened. "I'm okay. Just waiting out some dizziness. I love when you call me Cass. Oh, thank you." Taking the glass of orange juice, she took several sips. "My mouth is so dry."

"What time did you go take your shower?" Thomas asked, taking the glass from her to set it on her night stand.

"I woke just after ten, so shortly after that."

"Thank God, you didn't black out in the shower." The thought of what could have happened clutched onto his heart with a painful squeeze.

"He was here," Cassie said suddenly. "Eddie came into the washroom while I was showering. I saw him; he looked so alive."

"Shh, now, don't upset yourself." Lovingly, he stroked her hair, worry filling him. He couldn't lose her. He couldn't lose another woman he loved.

"There was a gunshot, and he ran from the room. I grabbed a towel and ran after him—"

Discovery in Passion

"You ran after him. Jesus, Cass." Any other woman would have locked herself in the room and cowered in the corner. But not his Cassie. She was brave.

"He's dead; he wasn't going to hurt me. I saw him in his room again, dead. He shifted his head and looked at me...and, well, that's about all I remember."

"You were lying on that floor, unconscious, for over an hour. Sweet Jesus!" Taking her in his arms, he ran a hand along her back, vowing never to leave her alone again.

"I'm okay, Thomas. He didn't do it."

He would keep her safe at any cost. "I don't want you staying here alone anymore."

"Don't start on that, again. Did you hear what I just said? He didn't do it."

"Do what?"

"Eddie Talbot didn't kill his family. He was in the washroom when the first bullet went off. Oh—" Cassie pushed from the bed and ran to the washroom.

Thomas waited for her by the washroom door and knew what he had to do.

This time he would not wait until it was too late.

Chapter 19

"I can manage this on my own, thank you." Cassie kissed Thomas quickly before she stood. She'd given in to him and agreed to have herself checked out at the local clinic, but she didn't need him helping her to the exam room. "You're sweet for caring, but I'll be okay."

Cassie left him with a frown on his lips and followed the nurse to the examination room. She sat on the examination table as the nurse instructed and waited for the doctor to show up. Cassie supposed she should have her records sent over from her regular doctor. She was due for her annual check-up, and it would be better if the new doctor had her records.

Cassie made a mental note to call her doctor back home and have the records sent over.

When the door opened to an elderly looking man in a white coat, she hoped there was more than one doctor in the clinic. She really did prefer a female.

"Good afternoon, Miss Evans. I'm Dr. Bowman."

"Pleased to meet you." She smiled politely, feeling slightly uneasy with the elderly man.

He flipped open her chart and read as he spoke. "So you've been having tummy problems." He lifted his head and smiled at her and the tension began to melt. "How long have you been feeling ill?"

"Since last night. I think I ate some bad ice cream."

Clucking his tongue, he stepped towards her and took her hand in his to check for her pulse. "Pulse is good. Have you been vomiting?"

"Yes."

"Diarrhea?"

"Nope."

"Dizziness?" He looked into her eyes, then pulled out a tongue depressor and his tiny pen light.

"Yes." She opened her mouth, and as he examined her throat, she couldn't help but notice the wrinkles beside his eyes. They made him look debonair. Men always looked better with wrinkles than women did. It just wasn't fair.

"How long has the dizziness been bothering you?"

She actually had to think about that. "A few weeks actually." She watched the dial moving while he checked her blood pressure. She had no idea what it meant, but it looked cool.

"Diabetes run the family?"

"No." Now he was worrying her.

"Have you injured your head recently?"

"No." She was beyond worry now.

"Have you ever blacked out?"

"Yes, I did, earlier this morning. You're worrying me, Doc."

Dr. Bowman smiled and those wrinkles danced at the corners of his eyes. "Just the usual questions. I think it might be a bout of mild food poisoning or the flu. Stick to clear liquids, broths and soups, plenty of water and juice, and you can take these to help calm that bubbly tummy." He sat in the chair and began writing on his prescription pad. "It's an anti-nausea med and should help a great deal. If the nausea gets worse or lasts longer than a week, come back in and see me.

He stood and held the prescription out to her. "Thanks, Doc."

"You just moved here, didn't you?"

"Two months ago." Cassie took the prescription, tucked it in her purse.

"Welcome. I'm assuming you'll need a doctor. I don't do a full time practice any longer. I'm getting too old to work that many hours." He smiled. "But there are two other doctors here that would be more than willing to help you out. Just ask Rachael at the desk to book you an appointment to get to know them."

"Thank you, Doctor Bowman." And as he left the room Cassie thought how silly she'd been in feeling uneasy with him. He was as sweet as pie.

~

"Could be food poisoning or the stomach flu," Cassie explained to Thomas while they walked to his truck. For a man with his wealth, she was surprised that he drove a beat up 1979 Ford truck.

"I'll fill the prescription for you after I settle you into bed."

"I can get my own prescription." She was feeling much better. Hopefully, the food poisoning had passed.

"I don't mind, and you really should rest."

Cassie stopped him by taking his arm in her hand. "Really, Thomas, I'm okay." Seeing the worry in his eyes, it suddenly dawned on her. "I'm such a fool. This must remind you a bit about your mom. I'm sorry, Thomas; I don't mean to make you worry."

He took her in his arms, and she felt so at home.

"Why don't we both get my prescription, and that way you can keep an eye on me." Satisfied with that, he took her hand in his and walked down the block to the drugstore. It took twenty minutes to fill her prescription, and while they waited, Thomas loaded his arms with juice and clear broth and anything else that lacked in taste. She had a moment to sneak a chocolate bar when he wasn't looking and hoped he wouldn't see her pay for it when she got her prescription. Despite her queasy stomach, she was dying for a chocolate bar.

Thomas paid for his groceries while she paid for her stuff, which meant he hadn't seen the bar. Tucking it in her purse for later, Cassie met him at the door. "Ready?"

Her eyes welled up when he handed her one long stemmed red rose. "Oh, Thomas, that is so sweet of you."

"I wanted to get you a huge bouquet, but I haven't had time."

"This is better." It had more meaning, Cassie thought. And she very nearly said the three little words she thought she would never say. Cassie suddenly felt her heart swell,

Discovery in Passion

and she knew she had fallen in love.

Sniffling back her tears, she swung her arm around his waist and walked with him to his truck.

~

By the time they arrived at her house, Cassie was past the teary-eyed emotions and well on her way to annoyance. He was demanding she stay at his place. Demanding, not suggesting or offering, demanding.

"Only for a few days, Cass, that's all I ask."

She pushed the gate open to her front yard, ready to make a stand. "And then those few days will lead to another few days and a few more... "

"So what if they do?"

Stopping short on the sidewalk that led to her front door, Cassie looked up at Thomas. "Are you asking me to move in with you?"

"Maybe I am."

Her brow lifted, and she let out a long breath. "We haven't known each other that long yet."

"We're practically inseparable now. Either I stay at your place, or you stay at mine. What's the difference?"

"You still have your place, and I have mine. It's too soon, Thomas."

"Oh, oh, lovers' quarrel."

Both Thomas and Cassie turned to the deep voice coming from Thomas' property. The first thought in Cassie's mind was, *wow*. He was tall; he was blond, and he looked like he had just stepped out of a magazine. His face was soft, his mouth curving up at the sides in a natural smile, and he had the bluest eyes she had ever seen on a man.

The black leather bomber jacket he wore made him look both dangerous and sexy.

"Vic?" Thomas said.

"In the flesh, pal. Did I interrupt a quarrel?"

"No. What the hell are you doing here?"

"What, no hugs? I missed you, too, pal." Pulling out a

cigarette, Vic leaned lazily against the joining fence.

"When did you get in? And why didn't you tell me you were flying in?" Moving to the fence, Thomas held out his hand.

"Three hours ago. I thought I'd surprise you." Thomas took Vic's hand in a sturdy shake, snatching the cigarette from Vic's mouth with his other hand.

"Those will kill you."

"Yeah, yeah, you're a broken record. Well, are you gonna introduce us or what?" His eyes shifted to Cassie with a sly smile.

"I'm Cassie, and you must be the friend Thomas was telling me about." She moved to the fence and took his hand and was utterly shocked when he lifted it to his lips.

"Damn, Tom, how did you manage to snag such a beauty? Pleasure to meet you, gorgeous. Wanna dump this old fool and come be with a real man?"

"I'd hate to have to kill you when you've just arrived, Victor." Thomas snarled.

Cassie bit her lip from grinning. "It's nice to meet you, Vic."

"Oh honey, the pleasure is all mine."

"Victor." Thomas warned.

Smiling, Cassie turned to Thomas. "Why don't I grab the groceries from the truck, Thomas, and you and Vic can catch up."

"Thomas. Oh, Lordy, you must be one hell of a woman if he lets you call him that."

Cassie cocked her head to the side as she spoke. "Why is that?"

"Only his mommy was allowed to call him Thomas."

"I'll help you with the groceries, Cassie." Thomas shot Vic a nasty glare.

"I'm fine, Thomas. Really, it's only two bags. Go, be with your friend." She gave Thomas a kiss on the cheek, then hurried to the truck for the bags.

~

"Damn, Tom. She is hot."

Thomas drew his attention away from watching Cassie, to Vic with a frown. "Back off."

His hands in the air, Vic replied, "Backing off. Do I smell love in the air?"

"Here's the keys; let yourself in. I'll be right back." Turning, Thomas rushed back to Cassie.

"I said I could manage this alone." Cassie snapped at him.

"I know what you said." Thomas took the bags from her and headed to her house. "I don't like you staying by yourself."

"I'll be fine. I'm a big girl, Thomas." She took the bags from him.

"I know you are." He stopped her at the door. "I'm worried about you."

"All I plan to do is curl up on the sofa and watch some TV. But it's sweet of you to worry." Reaching up, Cassie kissed him quickly. "Now go, be with your friend."

Thomas stood on her stoop as she shut the door. He hated leaving her alone, but he knew if he pushed her too far, she would only shut him out permanently.

That was the last thing he wanted.

Walking away from her was incredibly hard, but Thomas vowed he would not leave her for long.

Chapter 20

"Well…"

"What?"

"Are you gaga in love with her?"

"Yes." It was a relief to be able to actually say it out loud.

"Damn." Sitting at the kitchen table, Vic ran a hand across his face. "She know it?"

"No."

"You gonna tell her?"

Thomas shrugged, pulled out two bottles of beer from the cooler.

"How does she feel about you?"

Thomas shrugged again.

"Okay, I know you well enough to know when you don't talk, your mind's working on overtime or you're worried. What's up?"

"She hasn't been feeling well lately." He handed Vic a beer, then took his to the living room to relax.

"How not well?" Vic followed.

"The flu or possibly food poisoning."

"And that worries you. Come on, Tom, everyone gets sick, doesn't mean it's the end of the world."

"I know, still…"

Vic sat down beside Thomas. "Look, what happened with your mom sucks big time, and if they'd have caught it sooner, she might still be here. But not every illness is severe or life-threatening."

"I found her passed out on the floor in her hallway this morning." Thomas fiddled with his beer in his hands, not really wanting it. "It brought back memories."

"I bet it did. If it's any consolation, I think your mom would be pleased with your choice of women this time around. She is very hot and nothing like your usual maidens of blah."

Thomas liked to think his mother would like Cassie.

"She's an incredible woman, like no one I've ever known before."

"Oh, yeah, you're in love." Vic tapped his bottle against Thomas'. "Now tell me, what's the sex like?"

"Not getting enough of your own, you need to live through me?" Thomas smiled. Vic was always good with brightening his mood. Vic had been by his side after his mother had died, helping with the arrangements, being there to listen. Thomas wasn't sure he'd have been able to handle it as well as he had if it hadn't been for Vic.

"You know I never get enough. Come on, spill."

Shaking his head, Thomas leaned back and stretched his legs out. "Not in this lifetime. Are you going to tell me why you're here?"

"Didn't you miss me?" Vic smiled, lifting the bottle to his lips.

"You're evading."

"I am not. I came for a visit. You sounded like you needed help, so here I am."

"What did you find out?"

Vic twisted the bottle in his hands while speaking. "Edward and Luanne Talbot were found shortly after their deaths, both succumbing to a single gunshot wound. Son, Eddie, was found in his room with a single gunshot wound to his head, gun found on the floor at his side. Nephew of deceased found them shortly after Eddie shot himself."

"Calvin Talbot."

"Yep. Case was determined to be murder-suicide."

"Was there a note left behind by Eddie?"

"Nope."

"Not usual for a suicide."

"Not every suicide leaves a note. Edward Talbot had defensive wounds, which means he fought with his assailant; Luanne did not. Both deaths were determined to have occurred at, or nearly, the same time," Vic concluded.

"Then what? He shoots his parents, and out of guilt blows his brains out?"

"Seems like."

Thomas scratched his head. "Question is, why did he kill his parents?"

"Reports stated that there was some conflict between the elder Edward and his son."

"But not with his mother?"

Vic shook his head. "Not in the report, at least. Why is this so important to you? The case is closed."

Standing, Thomas rested his beer on the coffee table before walking to the living room window. There had never been any secrets between him and Vic, but to tell him that his girlfriend thought her place was haunted, and he believed her, might be a bit too much for Vic to handle.

Or...he could go with it and deal with whatever came at him. Turning, Thomas faced his friend and let it roll. "Her house is haunted." The snort of laughter from Vic was completely expected. "And I've seen the proof."

"You're worrying me, pal."

"Edward Talbot was laying face up, his eyes wide, his chest covered in blood from the gunshot wound that entered right below his heart. His wife, Luanne, was beside him, her left arm draped over his abdomen; she was face down, gunshot to the face which blew out the back of her head." He saw it register on Vic's face. "Edward wore a faded red plaid shirt and dark blue jeans. He was wearing scarred work boots in tan. His hair was brown and graying at the temples. His wife—"

"How the hell do you know all of this?"

"I saw them."

"In the crime scene photos?"

"How the hell would I get the crime scene photos? In living color—well, they weren't alive—but it sure seemed like I was there. I saw them, Vic, on the floor in Cassie's house, and it scared the living shit out of me."

"Should I call a shrink?"

"I'm not crazy. How long have you known me?"

"Since we were two; so, twenty eight years." Vic supplied.

"Then you know I wouldn't lie to you about this. Her place is haunted by the Talbots."

"No fucking way."

Thomas simply nodded.

"Shit." Vic wiped a hand across his face. "Okay, this I have to see. But first, I need the little boy's room."

Thomas moved to the window, wondering how Cassie was doing and decided he needed to go over and make sure she was okay. He was about to call out to Vic and tell him he would be right back when he heard Vic let out a loud whoop.

"Jesus, man, you are one lucky son of a bitch."

"Where are you?" Thomas followed Vic's laughter and entered his office studio. And then he saw what his friend was preoccupied with. "Oh, shit."

"Sweet God, she is one fine looking woman. Damn, you're lucky."

Thomas hurried to the nude portrait of Cassie and quickly draped a cloth over it. "Stop drooling."

"Oh, I'm doing more than drooling, pal. I am so damn jealous. Does she have a sister?"

"No." He looked at Vic, his eyes narrowing "Stop thinking about her; just wipe her out of your mind."

"Can't. Oh, am I going to have pleasant dreams tonight."

"Victor," Thomas warned.

"Come on, one more peek." He reached out for the cloth and received a nasty slap to his hand. "Party pooper."

"Damn straight. She's mine, and don't you forget it.

~

She'd only had a brief cat nap, but upon waking, Cassie felt much better. Food poisoning/flu was no laughing matter. She felt absolutely zapped from it.

Slipping out of bed, she headed for the hallway and stopped cold at seeing the figure of Eddie Talbot step up the last step and turn to the washroom. Her heart was hammering so hard in her chest it was making her lightheaded. Cassie took a couple of deep breaths and slowly inched closer. The sound of the gunshot jolted her, and when Eddie flew out of the bathroom, she nearly screamed.

There was another shot, and this time she did scream.

"What have you done?"

The voice was so low, so real, she thought for a brief moment Thomas had come into her house. But it was the next words spoken that made her realize otherwise.

"You killed them? What the fuck? You killed them."

Cassie raced to the stairs, but by the time she made it to the last one, Eddie was gone. She stood silent, only the sound of her labored breath could be heard as she stared into the emptiness of her living room.

When her back door opened, she nearly jumped out of her skin.

"I thought you'd be sleeping."

Cassie twisted to Thomas, wide-eyed, and swallowed the lump in her throat.

"Cass? Are you okay?"

"Eddie was just here, I saw him. He walked into the washroom; there was a gunshot, then another, and he ran down the stairs. I heard him talk to someone. He said, 'You killed them.'"

"Damn it. I knew I shouldn't have left you alone here."

"He didn't do it. He didn't kill his parents. Someone else was in the house."

"You're looking pale, Cass; you need to sit down." Taking her in his arms, he led her to the sofa.

"Where's your friend?" Her stomach was feeling a tad queasy, and Cassie was glad she was sitting.

Discovery in Passion

"Back at my place. I wanted to check on you. I want you to come home with me, now, Cass."

"Thomas—"

"Damn it, Cass. You're sick; you don't need to deal with this now."

"I'm not running away from it," she insisted, her voice low.

"You're not running away from it. Christ, think logically, Cass."

"I am thinking logically. He has never hurt me. I'm not afraid of him, so why should I leave."

"Am I interrupting?"

Both Thomas and Cassie turned to Vic, who stood in the doorway between the dining room and living room.

"Yes."

"No," Cassie insisted, shooting Thomas a nasty glare. "This conversation is over."

"The hell it is."

"I don't usually get involved in lovers' quarrels, but I think I'll make an exception this time. You both look like you need time to cool down, so I'll just jump in here. Cassie, I hear this place is haunted."

"Not a good time, Vic."

"It's a perfect time." Cassie dismissed Thomas and stood to speak to Vic. "Yes it is." She was prepared for the skepticism.

"That's what Tom tells me. I just need to know one thing."

"What is that?" Cassie asked.

"Why aren't you running away screaming?"

Cassie let out a huff. She should have expected as much from a friend of Thomas. Of course he would be on his friend's side. "Because it's my home." She turned her back on Thomas' grunt.

"Still…I'd be freaked."

"I was at first, but it's getting easier. He's trying to tell me something."

"Who is?" Vic inquired.

"Eddie."

"Yeah, and what's he trying to tell you?" Vic asked, lighting a cigarette.

"That he's innocent."

Chapter 21

Cassie watched while Vic drew lazily on his cigarette and wondered what he thought about what she'd said. She knew Thomas was fuming behind her and ignored his grunting as she waited for Vic's response.

"What makes you think that?" Vic asked, blowing out a long stream of smoke.

"Because he was in the washroom when the first gunshot rang out. He was on his way down when the second went off. And...I heard him talking to someone when he came down the stairs."

"You heard him talking to someone?"

"Yes." She crossed her arms over her chest.

"Not to be a complete ass, but you do know he is dead."

Her jaw clenched, Cassie spoke. "Yes. Look, I know what this must sound like to you, but I'm not delusional. I know what I saw—see—and what I heard. Eddie Talbot's spirit is here, and he wants me to make things right."

"I've never been a believer of reincarnation, spirits, Big Foot and all that sort of crap," Cassie let out a long sigh as he continued. "But I know my friend, and if he says he's seen a ghost—"

"Ghosts," Thomas corrected.

"Ghosts, then it must have happened. His description was pretty damn accurate to the crime scene photos," Vic reassured Cassie. "Why don't you tell me exactly what you saw and heard."

They sat in Cassie's living room while she explained what it was she saw and heard. Thomas sat quietly beside her; Vic nodded occasionally while she spoke.

After Cassie finished, Vic stood, opened her front door and tossed his cigarette outside. When he came back, his face was sober. "Looks like I'm going to be doing some investigating."

"Is that why you came here?"

"Not entirely." Vic smiled at Cassie. "I wanted to see the woman that my friend is smitten with."

"Victor," Thomas warned with a sharp look.

"And..." Cassie asked, waiting.

"You're hot; I mean really hot, and not Tom's usual type."

"Victor."

He waved Thomas off with a quick sweep of his hand as he moved to Cassie. "But that's not a bad thing. If you could have seen his other dates,"

"If you wanna keep walking on those legs, Victor; you'll shut your mouth now." Thomas snarled.

"Oh, now I have to know." Vic had her attention now.

Smiling, Vic continued. "Spinsters, the kind with mousy hair tied back, reading glasses falling down their nose and dowdy looking clothing."

"Really." Cassie was amused.

"And quiet, those 'yes' kind of girls. 'Oh, Tom, I'll do whatever you say' all the while batting owl eyes. It was sickening."

"You're dead." Standing, Thomas glared at his friend.

Vic backed away but he didn't stop. "You, on the other hand, shit, you have everything they didn't have and more. No way would any of his other dates have allowed him to paint them nude, and thank you, God, for that."

"What?" Cassie spun on Thomas, her eyes wide.

"You are dead." Thomas took a step towards Vic but Cassie stopped him with a firmly placed hand on his chest.

"You let him see the portrait?" She wasn't sure if she was more mortified or pissed.

"I did not." Thomas shot Vic a deadly glare. "He happened into my studio."

"Why wasn't it covered? Oh, my God, he saw—" She spun around. "You saw—oh, I need to sit." Dropping down on the sofa, Cassie laid her head on her knees and told herself just to breathe.

"It's not going to be easy telling your parents and sister that you're dead, but they'll get over you," Thomas warned Vic as he sat down beside Cassie.

"What's the biggie? It's not like I'm the only one going to see it. When you put it in the gallery, everyone will be looking at her."

Cassie whimpered, and Thomas stroked her back with his hand. "It's not being displayed."

"Get out."

"I wish you would." Thomas glared at his friend.

"Why the hell not? That is a masterpiece, and you haven't had many of those lately."

"Vic, I think it would be best if you left," Thomas advised, continuing to stroke Cassie's back.

"Okay, I'm outta here."

"Stay out of my studio," Thomas called out to Vic as he left.

"You have to burn it."

"What?"

Cassie lifted her head, reminding herself to breathe. "The portrait, you have to burn it."

"The hell I will."

"I don't want anyone else seeing it. I never should have posed for it. What was I thinking?"

"You were thinking to seduce me." He smiled, running a hand along her face. "I'll keep it covered, but I refuse to give it up. Vic was right; it is a masterpiece, simply because there has never been anything as beautiful as you."

Her eyes lifted to him looking a little glossy. "You are going to make me cry."

Cupping her face in his hands, Thomas kissed her quivering mouth, long and slow, before releasing her. "Now pack some things."

"What?" She pulled back, her mind clearing.

"Make sure you pack enough for at least a week."

She stood, waiting out the flash of dizziness before

placing her hands on her hips. "You're infuriating." Taking her leave, Cassie stomped off to the dining room.

"Where are you going?" Thomas asked, following her.

"Away. I need some air." Grabbing her purse, she pushed through the back door and out into the warm sun.

"You're not well enough to drive on your own."

"The hell I'm not. I'm not dying. I have food poisoning. I'll be fine." Cassie stomped across her lawn to her garage. She needed some time away from him before she strangled him.

"Cass—" She slammed the garage door, cutting off his words..

He had no right to demand anything of her.

~

Why were men so pigheaded? They hadn't progressed much since the days when they would beat their chests and grunt, "Me man. You woman. You obey man."

Shutting the door to her shop, Cassie continued to fume.

How dare he demand she leave her home? It was her home, and nothing was going to make her leave it. And she wasn't so helpless that she needed him to cater to her. She had food poisoning, nothing more, and she would get over it. Her stomach was feeling better already.

Seeing the many shelves Thomas had made for her and all the intricate detail he'd put into them softened her heart, but not enough to forgive him for being a Neanderthal.

Her father was the same way with both her and her mother. Always doting on them, worrying whenever they got the slightest sniffle or body aches or pains. And her mother—God love her—fed off of it. Yet it drove Cassie nuts. Sure, she loved her father dearly. He was such a sweet man. But she liked to do things her way—hence the reason she'd been adamant about moving far away from her parents. She'd known they would have insisted on helping her start her business, and like always, she would have felt obligated to let them simply because she hated letting her family down.

Well, she was on her own now, and she was going to make the best of it. Even if it meant living in a haunted house. And if Thomas didn't like it, well, to hell with him.

Pulling up a metal framed chair, Cassie sat down and had a good cry.

She wasn't prone to crying jags, yet lately she couldn't seem to stop herself.

Being in love sucked.

Grabbing a tissue from her purse, Cassie sat alone in her shop, her heart aching as she wept for the man she loved. She wanted to be with him now, in the worst way. But that would mean she was giving in to him.

She had something to prove, even if it meant dealing with the painful consequences of being alone.

Chapter 22

Thomas was in a horrible mood. He'd spent the evening trying to contact Cassie, and when she hadn't responded to his calls, he'd gone to her place. When that got him nowhere, he'd driven to her shop where he was relieved to finally find her.

The relief was short lived and followed by sheer frustration when she refused to let him in. She'd glared at him through the glass and had even had the audacity to lift her middle finger at him when he'd demanded she open the door. And when he'd yanked on the door, insisting she open it, she'd threatened to call the cops on him.

Because he'd been sure she would carry through with it, he'd given in and had left. He spent the rest of the evening drowning his anger with beer.

"You know," Vic began, sitting next to him on the patio, "maybe if you came out and told Cassie how you felt instead of bullying her, she might be more receptive."

Thomas grunted a response and downed the remainder of his beer. He'd only told one other woman he loved her and that had been his mother. It wasn't easy to tell another woman those words, despite the ache he felt in his chest.

He'd spent a good part of the evening wallowing under the full moon, waiting for Cassie to return. Even when it started raining, he still sat and waited, and when she finally pulled up, he'd raced—maybe a bit too eagerly—to his fence to talk to her. She'd waved him off as she darted for her door.

Furious all over again, Thomas stomped his way into the house and into his studio. He spent the better part of the night throwing his anger onto canvas and by morning light, had three works of art he considered good enough to display.

He'd even titled one, *Women's Fury* and thought how

fitting it was that the fury was a storm with raging lightning zigzagging across the sky while the ocean below churned with deadly force.

He was on his third cup of coffee, still staring at his work, when Vic staggered into the room.

"Have you even been to bed? Oh, wow, someone's in a snit." Rubbing his chin, Vic admired the artwork before him.

"No." Leaving the cup on the table with his supplies, Thomas took a step back and moved to the left to get another angle on the painting. It was good; the best work he'd done in...four years at least.

"If this is what love does to a man, I want no part of it. Any coffee left?"

"Yes." Grabbing his cup, Thomas stomped out of the room.

"Why don't you just tell her you love her, throw her down on the bed and fuck her brains out?" Vic stated while he poured coffee.

"Not everything can be solved with sex."

Vic snorted and nearly choked on his coffee. "Please, what are you trying to do, kill me? Give her some time to cool down. You could use some cooling off yourself. If you go over there looking like this, she'll boot your ass from here to eternity."

"What's wrong with how I look?"

"Well, for one, you haven't shaved, and that crazed look in your eyes will probably scare the living shit out of her. And nothing worth resolving was ever done with rage. Calm down before you talk to her."

"Since when have you become the voice of logic?" Grabbing a muffin from the breadbox, Thomas smeared some cream cheese over it and bit half off. Vic was the love 'em and leave 'em type. He couldn't remember a time Vic had dated a woman for more than two days. Vic certainly had no place giving relationship advice.

"I'm just saying. If you love her as much as I think

you do, you'll only scare her off by being a brute. Buy her some flowers, go in groveling, and she'll be putty in your hands."

"But she's wrong."

"Oh, pal, if my mother taught me anything, it's that women are never—let me emphasize that just a bit more—NEVER wrong."

"She shouldn't be staying at her place alone. She's sick, and seeing dead people isn't going to help her get better."

"Oh, man, listen to this conversation. If anyone was to hear us, they'd call the men in white to take us both away. Have the ghosts ever hurt her—I can't believe I'm saying this." Shaking his head, Vic refilled his cup.

"No, but—"

"Then what's the biggie?"

"She shouldn't be alone while she's sick."

"Has she never been sick before?" Vic asked with sarcastic surprise. "Jesus, she's a miracle."

"Get bent."

"She's a big girl, Tom; she can take care of herself. Not everyone is your mom."

"If I had insisted she go see a doctor when she first started feeling sick, she might—"

"Stop doing this to yourself, Tom. How could you have known? You couldn't. People get sick every day; that doesn't mean they'll die. Cassie has food poisoning, isn't that what you said?"

"Yeah, but—"

"And that too shall pass. If you love her, give her space or you'll drive her away. Now, I'm going to go into town and do some investigating."

"You have authority to do that?"

Vic chuckled, placing his cup in the sink. "Pal, I don't need authority to ask questions. Catch you on the flip side."

Taking his cup to the dishwasher, Thomas set it

beside Vic's before heading to the back door.

The hell he was going to give her space.

~

How long did it take to get over food poisoning? Her stomach rolling, Cassie sipped her water carefully, hoping the nausea subsided enough to keep the dry toast down she'd managed for breakfast.

Sitting at the kitchen table, Cassie could hear the birds chirping and smiled, thinking how they must be enjoying the fresh dew off the grass and the worms that had slithered their way to the surface.

And thinking about slithery worms did little to calm her stomach.

Cassie heard the sound of heavy boots on the wooden deck stairs, and before she could make it to the door to lock it, Thomas yanked it open. She growled at him as she spoke. "I didn't invite you inside."

"I don't give a damn. You look pale."

She jerked away when he reached out to her cheek. "I'm still mad at you, so back off."

"For what? Because I'm concerned about your health?"

"For being a demanding jerk." Her temper heating her face, Cassie spun on her heals and walked away.

"I wouldn't have to demand if you thought logically."

"I am thinking logically." She rinsed her plate off and set it in the dishwasher.

"The hell you are. I find you out cold on the hallway floor, and you think you're capable of taking care of yourself."

"One time deal, buddy." Cassie moved through the kitchen, doing her best not to look at him.

"It could happen again. Do you have any idea what could happen to you? You could have hit your head on the wall, fallen down the stairs—"

"But I didn't," she insisted, trying to ignore the fact that he'd followed her to the living room.

"This time. What about next time?"

"Jesus, Thomas, listen to yourself. What do you plan to do; watch me for the rest of my life?"

"Yes."

Her eyes went wide. "Are you for real? Do you know how close to stalking that sounds?"

"I'm not stalking you, damn it, I love you," he blurted out

Cassie paused, stepped back and took in what he'd said to her. "Well, I love you, too, you brute, but that doesn't mean I need you watching me every second of the damn day." Planting her hand on his firm chest, she gave him a hard shove.

He grabbed her wrist. "I wouldn't need to watch you if you came to live with me instead of living in a haunted house."

"It's my house, haunted or not." She tried to yank her hand free, but his grip was much too tight. "Back off."

"I'm not going to lose you."

"You won't fucking lose me. Jesus." She yanked again, only this time he jerked her towards him. Her blood was suddenly boiling, and it had nothing to do with anger and everything to do with lust.

Her eyes focused on his, Cassie pushed him back, causing him to bump into the bottom stair and tumble backwards to land in a sitting position.

"I'm still pissed at you, but God have mercy, I'm turned on by it." She dove on top of him, spreading her legs and straddling him. With eager hands, she yanked at his zipper, desperate to free him.

"Nothing was ever resolved with sex," Thomas panted, yanking her robe open, then devoured her awaiting breasts.

"Oh, God." Her body quivered when his tongue slid over her erect nipples. "Fuck logic." Finally freeing him, she positioned his penis, lowering down, she engulfed him. "Oh, sweet heavenly God."

Discovery in Passion

While he devoured each breast, Cassie rode him vigorously, moving her hips back and forth. His hands clamped onto her hips, urging her on, and she was happy to oblige. She bounced on him, feeling crazed and wondering if she might fall over the edge if she didn't receive the final release.

Her hands threading through his hair, she held his head in place as he suckled her breasts, and when the ripple of pleasure struck her, she threw her head back and cried out as her body rippled with a tidal wave of an orgasm.

She collapsed against him, feeling him twitch inside of her and knew he too had felt the release. "I'm still pissed at you."

"Same goes."

"Bedroom?"

Without a word, he hoisted her up, then carried her to her bed where round two took place.

He pumped her good and hard, and she loved it. And when she thought she could give no more, he rolled her onto her belly, lifted her hips in the air and sent her screaming into her pillow. Her body pulsated with an orgasm that she could actually feel in every part of her body. When he'd spent himself, he released her, collapsing on the bed and drawing her down beside him.

"Angry sex is pretty damn good."

Thomas laughed, pulling her against his chest. "I agree with you wholeheartedly."

"I'm not moving in with you."

He opened his eyes to look down at her. "Cass—"

"Only because I'm not ready for such a big commitment yet." She lifted her head and thought how foolish it was that she should be terrified of committing. He was everything she could ask for and more. "I need some time, okay?"

He kissed her head, then drew her down to him. "Okay."

Smiling, she drifted off to sleep, feeling completely content.

Victory was hers.

Discovery in Passion

Chapter 23

Her shop was coming along nicely. Though, when Cassie thought about opening in less than two weeks, it scared the hell out of her. Thomas had worked hard at getting all the shelves and cabinets built for her, and they looked fantastic. He really had a talent for creating, among other things.

He'd agreed to give her time and not pressure her into moving in with him, but he rarely left her alone when she was in her house, and he often spent the nights with her. She felt more comfortable staying in her place while Vic was staying with Thomas. Not that she didn't like Vic; in the two weeks since he'd shown up, she'd grown quite fond of him. But having him under the roof when she wanted to make crazy monkey love with Thomas was a bit unnerving.

So they stayed at her house more often than at Thomas'. They didn't just have sex—but, oh, when they did, they rocked the foundation. They also enjoyed being in one another's company. When she wasn't working to get her shop up and running, they spent time watching TV or sitting out on the deck with Vic, enjoying the cool evening breeze and a casual glass of wine.

There wasn't a day that went by that the words "I love you" weren't said. It was easy for her to tell Thomas she loved him now that Cassie found it just slipped from her lips without thought.

And he loved her just the same.

It seemed even the spirits understood the love between them. They'd settled down quite a bit over the past few weeks. Not that Cassie didn't still see Eddie—she did—but not as often as she had.

Thomas, on the other hand, was often startled by the visions of Eddie's parents sprawled out on the living room floor in a pool of blood. He hadn't told her any of the details, but she'd overheard him talking with Vic, and it had sent her scurrying to the washroom.

It annoyed her that she was still feeling queasy and she wondered how long it took to get over a bout of food poisoning. Giving in, Cassie made an appointment with the female doctor at the clinic, to find out if there was anything she could do to make herself feel better before her grand opening.

"Good afternoon, Miss Evans. I'm Dr. Lyndal."

"Pleasure to meet you, Doc, and, please, call me Cassie." Dr. Lyndal was a tall thin woman who looked like she didn't have an ounce of fat on her body. Her face was long, thin-boned with deep set blue-green eyes. Her mouth was wide as she smiled and held out her hand for Cassie to shake.

"Cassie it is, then. I hear you're still not feeling up to par. I checked into your file and saw that Dr. Bowman thought it might be food poisoning and sent you home with an anti-nausea med." The doctor lifted smiling eyes to Cassie. "And here you are, still ill. Tell me your symptoms."

"I'm queasy all the time. My stomach feels like I have a batch of angry butterflies fighting for territory. I'm dizzy, and if I stand up too quickly or bend over and stand up, I have to watch that I don't pass out."

"Hmm. And this has been going on for...over a month now." She looked up from the folder. "When was your last period?"

"Um...let me check." Opening her purse, Cassie pulled out her date book and flipped through the pages. "Well, that can't be right."

"What?"

"I must have forgotten to mark it down."

"When was your last period?"

Cassie looked up, her head cocked to the side. "Well this says I haven't had one in two months, but I'm sure..." Her brow furrowed in thought. "I must have had one since I moved here."

Discovery in Passion

"Can you remember having one?"

Cassie let out a breath. "No." Even racking her mind she couldn't think of having it since she'd moved.

"Are you having sex?"

Cassie gave the doctor a baffled look. "Yes."

"Do you use protection?"

"I'm on the pill."

"Condoms?"

"No." She let out a long breath. "You're not thinking—"

"That you might be pregnant? You betcha I am. But let's not jump the gun until we do the test. You wait here, and I'll have the nurse take a blood and urine sample."

Cassie sat with her jaw open as Dr. Lyndal left the room. She couldn't be pregnant. She was on the pill. It had to be something else. Her mind working on the thought that she might be pregnant; she barely noticed the needle when the nurse drew her blood. And as Cassie gave a urine sample, her mind was still on over time.

When Dr. Lyndal walked in with her file, Cassie pounced. "Well, what did the test say?"

"Positive. You are definitely pregnant."

"No!"

"And apparently not ready for it."

"How? How can I be pregnant? I'm on the pill."

"The pill isn't one hundred percent effective. We can look into alternatives."

"For the pill?" What good did that do her now that she was pregnant?

"For the pregnancy. If you're not ready—"

"Oh, I am so not ready." Cassie laughed, having a hard time coming to terms with what she'd just learned.

"Then we can look into—"

"I'm having this baby," she said, stopping what she was afraid the doctor had been about to say.

"Oh, alright. I just thought—"

"I'm scared shitless, don't get me wrong. A baby,

wow, big responsibility. But I'm not giving it up." Cassie's hand clamped protectively onto her belly.

"Great. Then we need to get you started on prenatal vitamins and—"

"I've been drinking. And I was taking those anti-nausea pills the other doctor gave me. Oh, my God, what if I've hurt my baby?" Now she was terrified. What if she'd done something awful to harm her child? Her eyes welled up with the mere thought.

"Not to worry, the anti-nausea meds are harmless."

"But the wine, what about the wine? I've had wine."

"Wine is actually one of the safer alcohols, not that I am condoning drinking during your pregnancy, but in perspective, wine is okay."

"Oh, okay." Letting out a huge breath, Cassie felt marginally better.

Until she was in her car, and everything finally sunk in.

"Holy crap. I'm pregnant. Oh, crap, Thomas." Leaning her head on the steering wheel, Cassie tried not to hyperventilate.

How was she going to tell him she was pregnant?

~

Cassie was grateful to find her house empty when she returned. She wasn't quite ready to face Thomas yet. Kicking her heels off, Cassie made her way up the stairs, deciding a hot bubble bath was precisely what she needed.

The rain had started up while she'd been in the clinic and had brought a torrent of it since she'd left. By the time she ran from her garage to her house, Cassie had been drenched from head to toe.

Her damp toes left prints on the hardwood as she walked up the steps to the washroom. Stripping from her soaking clothing, she started the hot water, cooled it down just enough to feel comfortable, then added a capful of bubbles before slipping under the water.

It felt like heaven.

How was she going to tell Thomas? How was she going to tell her parents? Surely her family would think she'd completely lost her mind. Not only had she flown off to places unknown, but she'd bought a small house and was planning to open her own business to which she had no clue of what she was doing. But now, on top of it all, she was pregnant.

Cassie was pretty damn sure her father would insist she fly home immediately.

But she wouldn't. This was her home now; she had a life here and would soon have a baby.

Holy mother of God, she was going to have a baby.

Sliding down further under the soapy water, Cassie placed her hand over her flat belly. There was a tiny person inside, growing, forming. One she had created with the man she loved. It scared the hell out of her, and yet at the same time, she was giddy with excitement.

She was going to be a mom.

Cassie jumped when the bathroom door flew open, then let out a long sigh as Eddie enter the room. "Not now. I want some quiet me and my thoughts time."

But he didn't hear her, as usual, and bent over the sink to wash the grime from his face. The sound of the gunshot made her jump and as she sat up she watched Eddie dart from the room. She was prepared for the next gunshot.

"Great." Pulling the plug, Cassie slipped from her warm comfort and pulled a towel around her damp body. "So much for relaxing." She heard Eddie cry out, heard him accuse someone of murdering his family, and just as she stepped out of the washroom, Cassie caught sight of him in his room.

Something wasn't right, so she stepped into the room to get a closer look. He was lying over the desk, but there was no blood, no head wound. And there was no gun.

Cassie tried to piece it together, tried to figure out the

clues—and she knew they were clues that he was giving her. She'd just seen him in the washroom, then the first gunshot. Eddie ran from the room as the second gunshot rang out. He'd argued with someone, accused someone of killing his parents, and now he was lying over his desk, but there was no head wound.

How was that possible?

Cassie spun around when she heard the footsteps coming up the stairs and was surprised to see Eddie racing to the washroom. He looked like he'd just gotten home from work. But where? From the grease on his hands and coveralls, she would guess a garage.

She jumped at the first gunshot, berating herself for it, preparing for the second when Eddie raced down the stairs. Glancing back to his desk, he was no longer there. Baffled, Cassie stepped into the hallway just as he accused someone of killing his parents. Hearing a creak behind her, she shifted and saw Eddie lying over his desk. Again, no blood.

"I don't understand. How can you be unconscious but not dead?"

Cassie spun around as he raced into the washroom and blew out a long breath. "I know this part. You go to the washroom to wash your hands and face; the first gun goes off," She jerked a finger out as the first gunshot went off. "And then you race to the stairs and the next..." She slashed her hand out as the second gunshot went off. "You argue with someone and then you're here." Cassie turned to him. "I just don't get what you're trying to tell me."

Startled, she jumped back when his body lifted to a sitting position, though it looked like he was still out cold. Stepping back, Cassie bumped into the wall, watching what looked like someone carrying him, though there was no one besides her and Eddie in the room.

In reverse, Cassie watched him being carried by an invisible presence to the door, then they began to walk towards the desk. He was draped over the desk, his left hand lifted and a gun appeared.

Standing in shock, she watched as the gun was held to his head by his own hand but clearly by someone else's.

Cassie let out a scream when the gun went off and blood splattered against the wall beside him.

Turning, she ran for her room, her towel falling in her wake as she dove into bed.

Pulling the pillow over her head, she wept.

Chapter 24

The house was so quiet that, for a moment, Thomas thought maybe Cassie wasn't home. But then he saw her shoes lying carelessly on the floor.

"Cass? You here?" Getting no response, he panicked and rushed through the dining room and living room in search of her. Coming up empty, Thomas took the stairs in twos, his booted feet clambering as he raced up the stairs. When he saw the towel lying on the hallway floor, his panic level rose. Finding her curled up in her bed, completely naked eased the worry but also managed to stir every primal urge inside of him.

But he realized that if she'd taken to her bed, it was because she'd been either tired or sick. He couldn't jump her and have wild and crazy sex if she was feeling sick.

With a sigh of regret, Thomas moved to the bed and instead of rolling her over and having his way with her, settled in beside her and stroked her back.

Cassie rolled over, stretched, and he was lost. When her hand slid down over his pants to rest on his rapidly expanding hard-on, he thought he might lose his mind. "You're killing me, sweetie," he whispered, reminding himself just to breathe through his arousal.

Hell, like that was working.

When she lifted her naked leg and laid it over his, her breasts pressing to his side, he actually groaned.

Be a gentleman, Thomas, be a gentleman.

"I want you," she whispered in a low, sleepy yet incredibly sexy tone.

And it was all he needed to take what he wanted. Rolling her onto her back, he took her mouth in a hot hungry kiss while his hands wandered that luscious body of hers. She was ripe for his taking, and her breasts spoke volumes. When she spread her legs, inviting him to touch, he did. She moved for him as he massaged her, as he drew out the juices of her arousal. Her mouth was hot against his, her tongue inviting him to take more.

And so he did.

Plunging a finger inside, he drove her to insanity as she pumped her hips, her fingers tugging at the zipper of his jeans.

"Give me," she panted and freed him.

She whimpered when he pulled his hand free to tug his jeans down. Taking her hips in his hand, he hoisted her up, then plunged. The cry she let out was both surprise and pleasure, and as he pumped himself into her, she arched her back and released a wave of erotic juices in her orgasm that sent him completely over the edge.

"Good morning, sleepy baby." Her lips were warm and swollen, and he could easily kiss them all day long.

"Baby. Oh, my God." She gave him a shove and when he wouldn't budge, she pushed a little harder. "Get off of me; you're too heavy. Oh, crap, I hope its okay. Damn it."

Rolling to his side, completely baffled, he watched Cassie lift her bedside phone and dial.

"I need to talk to Dr. Lyndal, now. Yes it's urgent."

Thomas sat up. "Cass?"

"Dr. Lyndal. I just had sex. Is that safe; did I harm the baby?"

"Baby?"

"You're sure? It was kinda rough? Okay, okay, thanks." She hung up the phone and let out a long breath.

"Baby?"

Cassie's eyes snapped towards Thomas. "Oh, crap, that was stupid; that wasn't how I planned on telling you. Damn it." She slapped her head.

"How about you start from the beginning and tell me what the hell is going on?"

Letting out a long breath, Cassie sat up and began, "I'm pregnant."

Thomas sat up, running a hand over his face, trying to comprehend what she was telling him.

"This really wasn't how I pictured telling you, not that I really pictured it—actually, I didn't have a clue how I was going to tell you. I only found out this morning. Talk to me, Thomas; you're scaring the hell out of me."

He looked at Cassie, she was so incredibly beautiful and very naked, and all he could think was, *She's having my baby*. "Did I hurt you? Did I hurt the baby? Jesus, I never should have taken you with such force. Damn it, we should get you in to the doctor's and make sure everything is okay." Slipping from the bed, he hoisted her into his arms, hurrying from the room.

"Thomas—"

"Shh, baby, just relax, breath, and if you feel any cramps, just stay calm."

"I'm fine, Thomas."

"Okay, just stay that way. Damn, I'm an idiot."

"Um, honey. If we go out that door like this, we'll be arrested."

"What?" He shifted her to yank open the back door.

"Sweet Jesus." Vic spun around, shielding his eyes.

Cassie squealed, curled herself into Thomas to hide at least some of her nudity. "Upstairs, Thomas, now! Clothes," Cassie demanded.

Thomas looked down, saw her nudity, then realized he wasn't wearing a stitch either and quickly spun towards the stairs.

"What the hell were the two of you going to do, fuck in the back yard in broad daylight?" Vic called out as Thomas rushed Cassie up the stairs.

Thomas dropped Cassie on the bed, giving her a baffled look when she burst into laughter. "What's so funny?"

"You, me, this." She held her belly while she laughed.

"Are you having contraction?"

"Oh, Lord, Thomas," She laughed even more. "I'm not far enough along to have contractions. Oh, this is too

Discovery in Passion

funny."

"I don't see the humor in it." Thomas yanked on his jeans, careful not to catch anything in the fly as he drew the zipper up. She was pregnant, and he'd been an animal with her, and all she could do is sit there and laugh.

"I'm okay; the doctor said sex is fine during pregnancy. Oh, Lord." She panted with her laughter.

"Should I leave? Are the two of you going at it up there?" Vic asked.

"No." Thomas yelled down to Vic then looked over at Cassie. "You're not in any pain?"

"No, well, my belly from laughing, but I'm fine; we're fine." Her laughter stilled slowly as Cassie looked up at him. "I'm pregnant, Thomas."

He sat down beside her on the bed and let out a long breath. "Holy fuck."

"Yeah, pretty much what I thought, too."

"I think I'll head back to your place, Tom. When the two of you are done going at it, come by, and I'll tell you what I found out about the Talbot murders," Vic called up to them.

"Oh, my God, he saw me naked." Lifting off the bed, Cassie raced to her closet for some clothes.

"You're really pregnant?"

Grabbing a navy dress, Cassie nodded. "I'm really pregnant. I didn't do it on purpose, if that's what you're thinking."

He lifted angry eyes. "Don't be stupid, of course I wasn't thinking that. If anything, it's my fault. I never used a condom, and I never once asked you if you were on the pill."

"I am on the pill, but it's not one hundred percent effective. I'm keeping the baby, Thomas, and you don't have to worry about responsibility. I can raise it on my own."

"The hell you will. This is my child as much as it is yours. We'll raise it."

"I don't want you to think you have to out of obligation."

He heard the anger in her voice and understood why she might be feeling defensive. Standing, he walked to her, taking her hands in his. "I love you; I love this child we created and neither of you are an obligation to me."

"I don't want you to regret this and feel stuck."

"Oh, Cass, how could you even think that." He leaned down to kiss her quivering lips.

"You said it was your fault."

"That wasn't what I meant, though. Responsibility is what I should have said. I'm as responsible for the pregnancy as you are."

"Do you want it, though?"

He cupped her delicate face in his hands, seeing the sweetness behind the utter beauty. "Anything that's a part of you I want. We created her or him, and nothing could be more beautiful than that."

"Oh, now you're making me cry."

Scooping her into his arms, he held her while she sniffled onto his shoulder.

~

"All done with your dinner time sexcapades?" Vic asked the instant Thomas entered the house.

He simply waved him off and headed for the phone.

"She looks even better in person."

"Wipe my girlfriend's naked body from your mind, Victor, before I knock it out of you with my fist." Thomas gave his attention to the phone when the florist answered. "Yes, hello, I would like to order four—no, make it six dozen, pink long stemmed roses. Today. Okay, first thing tomorrow morning then. Yes, I would. In the card write, 'To my love. You've given me the greatest gift I could ever ask for. Love, Thomas.' I'll pay by credit card."

When Thomas replaced the phone, Vic spoke. "Six dozen, huh? She must be something alright."

"She's pregnant," Thomas blurted out, sinking down

onto one of the kitchen chairs. "I'm going to be a daddy."

"What? Get the fuck out of here." Sitting beside Thomas, Vic stared at him. "For real?"

"For real." And it was all sinking in. He was going to be responsible for a little human being. His child.

"Oh, Tom, Tom, Tom."

"I'm happy about this," he responded to Vic's shake of head.

"You purposely got her pregnant?"

"Hell no, but I'm glad she is. We're keeping the baby."

"And what if it doesn't work out between the two of you?"

"It will work out because we love each other."

"This is a big step."

"I know."

"You gonna marry her?"

"Of course I am."

"Well, then, I'm happy for you." Vic held his hand out; Thomas clenched it hard before pulling him in for a bear hug. "You'll make a great dad."

"Yeah, I will."

"And your mother would be happy for you."

He released Vic, his mind drifting to his mother. "I hope she would be."

"She would be. Her only baby having a baby and with a great woman at that. I like her, she's a great gal."

"Stop picturing her naked."

"Hard to stop when it's seared into my mind, and here's the lady in question. And damn, she's wearing clothes."

"Never discuss what you saw," Cassie warned Vic as she stepped through the door. "And if you ever speak of it again, I'll lop your dick off."

"Fucking shit, vicious broad." Vic clamped a hand over his crotch.

"Damn straight," she said with a smile.

"Would it be safe for me to give you a hug?"

"As long as your hands stay on my back."

"Oh, I really do like her," Vic said to Tom, standing to embrace Cassie. "Congrats, Mommy."

"Thank you. You told him already?"

"It just came out." Thomas smiled as he held his hand out to her. "You feeling okay?"

"As okay as a knocked up woman can feel. So, what do you have for me, Vic?"

"Loaded question, honey, but I'll behave." They sat around the table while Vic began. "Betty Talbot is one nervous broad. I thought for sure the woman was going to have a breakdown while I was questioning her. She didn't give me anything lucrative. Said she waited in the car while Calvin went inside for some camping gear. Neither of them heard the gunshots because they had their music too loud, which sounds like a bullshit line to me but..."

"She was quite nervous with me, too," Cassie added.

"Her hubby wasn't much better. The guy put on a good show with the grief, but he was as nervous as a prostitute in a church. Calvin claims to have entered right after the murders, saw the couple on the floor the instant he entered the back door."

"You can't see directly into the living room from the back door," Cassie supplied.

"That's what I said, but he had a quick response. He said he hadn't meant the instant he entered the house but when he'd entered the dining room instead."

Thomas leaned his elbows on the table. "Sounds like a line to me."

"You got that right, pal," Vic agreed and continued. "He also claims he only checked the bodies for a pulse, and when I questioned the fact that he was covered in blood, he became evasive."

"I don't understand."

"A person isn't saturated in blood, sweetie, by simply checking for a pulse," Vic supplied.

Discovery in Passion

"Oh, okay." Cassie motioned for Vic to continue.

"Betty also mentioned that her father put both her and Calvin in his car while he checked out the scene."

"Together?" Thomas inquired with a lift of his brow.

"Yeah. Big no no."

"Why is that a no no?" Cassie wanted to know.

"In any case, you don't put the witnesses together before asking questions. Gives them time to corroborate their stories, or fill in blanks. Everyone sees things differently. So Betty might have seen something Calvin hadn't, and being in the car, she could have told him what she saw, therefore, implanting it into his head. When he's questioned later, he could add what Betty saw as what he saw but not have enough detail, making him look guilty."

"Okay, I get it. What does all this mean, then?" Cassie asked.

"It means I think there was a cover-up, and Calvin knows more than he's saying."

"Wow." Cassie leaned back in her chair, placing a hand on her belly.

"What are you thinking, Vic?" Thomas inquired.

"I'm thinking maybe the wife is the one I should look into more."

"Why the wife?" Cassie wanted to know.

"Because she's hiding something."

Chapter 25

"Are you thinking the wife might have killed them all?" Cassie inquired.

"No, not the wife. She's too skittish. But I think she might be my link to finding out the truth. You want a beer?" Vic asked Thomas, lifting to refresh his.

"No thanks."

With a shrug, Vic got himself one.

"Calvin?"

Vic nodded to Thomas. "Bingo. He's the most suspicious. Now I have to figure out how I'm going to prove it."

"Eddie can help us do that," Cassie piped in, lifting to her feet to pour herself a cup of coffee.

"How is he going to do that when he's dead?" Vic asked.

"He keeps repeating the same act, trying to show me some clues—hey!" She frowned at Thomas when he took the cup out of her hand.

"Coffee's bad for the baby." He dumped it in the sink, then opened the fridge for the milk instead.

"How do you know that?"

"There's caffeine in it; caffeine is bad for babies. This is better."

Cassie looked down at the glass of milk and frowned. "I hate milk."

"Get used to it." Thomas pushed it at her.

"Wow, this is so much fun, and I hate to interrupt, but…" Vic shot them both an impatient look. "I can't use the word of the dead, Cassie. Anything you tell me about Eddie would be inadmissible in court."

"But there might be some clues in it that might lead you to something that could be used. Right?"

"Drink your milk." Thomas pushed the glass towards her, and Cassie snarled at him. She hated milk.

"A pregnancy runs for nine months, right? And

you're what...?"

"Two months, give or take."

"Great, that means for seven months, give or take, I'll have to listen to the two of you butt heads over this kid. Fun times." Vic lifted his beer in salute.

"You won't be here the full seven months, so you won't have to worry about it. And you could use some coffee instead of another beer." Taking Vic's half full beer; Thomas replaced it with a cup of coffee.

"Is he always this bossy?" Cassie asked. He seemed even bossier than usual.

"No, he's usually worse. Congratulations, he's all yours now. And back to the gritty business of death. Explain what Eddie keeps showing you, Cassie."

Cassie drew in a deep breath before she began. "He walks into the washroom, turns on the taps and starts to wash up. He's covered in grease, and he's wearing dingy green coveralls. The first gunshot goes off, and Eddie races from the washroom just as the second one goes off. I hear him talk to someone, saying, 'You killed them', then I see him in his room, lying over his desk. Dead. Only today, it was different." Her stomach rolled just thinking about it.

"You saw him today?"

She gave Thomas a nod.

"How was it different?" Vic interjected.

"See, that's why I don't want you alone in that house, and especially now that you're pregnant. You're moving in with me."

"We've already discussed this Thomas, and the answer is still no." There was that bossiness, again.

"You're carrying my child, which is the biggest commitment anyone could ever have. Why should you be freaked about moving in with me?"

"I need time to get used to it." Cassie insisted, her eyes narrowed at Thomas.

"I need my beer." Vic stood, took the one Thomas

had taken from him off the cupboard and leaned against the sink while Cassie and Thomas continued to argue.

"To the baby or to living with me?"

"Both."

"Lucky for you then that you have seven months, give or take." Both Cassie and Thomas shot Vic a nasty look. "Let's put this discussion on hold and finish the one about the dead guy trying to tell you something. Okay?"

"Later, Vic."

"No, now is good," Cassie snapped at Thomas, then gave her attention to Vic. "Today, when I saw him on his desk, he hadn't been shot. It looked like he was sleeping on his desk. And then..." Cassie swallowed, reminding herself she was strong enough to finish this. "You know when you rewind a video tape? Well, that's what it looked like. He was carried into his room, unconscious, and laid over his desk. Then...I saw his hand come up and the gun appeared. It was held at his head and...the gun went off." She swallowed the bile that rose in her throat from the memory.

"That's it. We're going to pack your things and move you in here," Thomas demanded.

"The hell we are."

"I am not letting you stay one more day in that house."

"It's my damn house and I'll stay there as long as I see fit to stay there."

"Why are you being so stubborn about this?"

"Why are you being such a Neanderthal?" Cassie countered.

"Boy, love is grand," Vic groaned.

"Shut up, Vic," they both said in unison.

"Me and my beer will be over here." With his beer in hand, Vic sauntered off towards the living room.

"It's not safe for you or the baby to stay there, Cassie."

"Neither of us is in danger. And I hate milk, and you

can't make me drink it." Standing, she dumped it down the drain.

"Great, not only are you willing to put my child in jeopardy over a stupid house, but now you're going to deny it nourishment."

Cassie's jaw dropped. "How dare you." Spinning on her heels, she left the house.

~

"Cass." Thomas jumped when she slammed the back door in her wake.

"Let her go." Vic advised when Thomas got up to go after her.

"Stay out of it, Vic."

"Sorry, no can do. Sit down, Tom."

"Don't push me."

Shaking his head, Vic did exactly that. One shove had Tom tumbling back towards a chair. "Stop being a pigheaded fool for one minute and listen to reason. You go over there in this kinda mood, and the only thing you'll accomplish is to drive her away from you. What you said was uncalled for."

Hanging his head, Thomas nodded. "I'm worried about her and the baby."

"I know you are, but you're also becoming obsessive. It was tough on you to lose your mother, and I feel for you on that, but what are you going to do? Cage Cassie and the baby up to prevent anything bad ever happening to them?"

"Don't be an ass."

"Same goes." Vic pulled up a chair and sat across from his friend. "I know you love her, but if you keep this up, you'll smother her. She's a special gal; you don't want to lose her."

"I know that."

"Then enjoy that love while you have it, but give her space. Why doesn't she want to live with you?"

Thomas stole the beer from Vic and took a gulp

before responding. "She's not ready for that big of a commitment."

"Okay, that does seem a little silly in hindsight, but she's a woman, and who the hell knows their logic. You can suggest she move in with you, but demanding...well, look what that got you." Vic took his beer back and continued speaking. "Its tough losing someone you love, and I get that, but if you keep pushing at Cassie you'll lose her for sure." He stood, placing a hand on Thomas' shoulder. "Think about it." He left Thomas and walked out the back door, lighting a cigarette.

~

Fuming mad, Cassie stormed into her house, slamming the door behind her. She paced the floor, furious with Thomas. How dare he accuse her of harming her baby. She'd do anything for this child.

Placing a hand on her now flat belly, Cassie felt the love for something she couldn't see or feel warm her heart. She loved this baby, whatever it was, even if its father was a bully.

When the telephone rang, she nearly jumped out of her skin. Laughing it off, she picked it up, responding with a friendly, "Hello."

"Darling, it's Mother. How are you doing?"

Glancing down at the hand that rested on her belly, Cassie grinned. "Funny you should ask that. How would you and Dad feel about becoming grandparents?"

Chapter 26

Thomas had given Cassie the night to herself, though it had nearly killed him. He'd lost count how many times he'd gotten up and walked to the door before coming to his senses. Okay, before Vic made him come to his senses.

The guy was worse than a father with his sharp hearing. Thomas had been so quiet, hoping not to wake Vic, but the guy had heard him anyway.

"Go back to bed." Vic told him each time, and on the last, at about five in the morning, he'd even threatened to handcuff him to the bed.

"It's my damn life," Thomas insisted, and had received a, "You won't have one if you break in there now and wake her up, demanding she listen to you. Go back to bed."

He'd listened and had lain in his bed, wondering if she and the baby were doing alright.

Now that it was morning, Thomas saw no reason he couldn't go over to Cassie's house and see her.

"It's barely eight in the morning. You'll wake her."

Startled at seeing his friend at the table—looking a little bleary eyed however—Thomas snarled at Vic, "I have a key, and I'll be quiet."

"Man, you are far gone. I need your help today, so keep your salami in your pants."

Gritting his teeth, Thomas replied, "Not everything is about sex, Victor."

Vic snorted a laugh. "Right, and she isn't knocked up. She'll keep a few more hours. I need your assistance."

"With what?" Mildly annoyed with his friend, Thomas grabbed a cup and poured himself some coffee.

"I want to have a chit-chat with the lady across the street. Since you've lived here for years, she'll probably feel more inclined to talk to me with a familiar face beside me."

"Why do you want to talk to her?"

"She's the only witness that might be able to give me some insight."

"It can wait a half an hour until I check on Cassie."

"Or, you can wait a half hour to check on her. Trust me, pal, I know something about women, and she'll still be pissed at you. Come on; let's go make friendly with the neighbors."

~

She hadn't slept well at all during the night. Stretching her sluggish body, Cassie slid from her covers and slipped into her robe. The room shifted on her, and she braced a hand on the wall. Now that she knew the reason for the dizziness, she wasn't as annoyed with it. There was a little creature in her belly making its mommy feel like crap.

God love her—or him.

Cassie trudged down the steps, rubbing her sleepy eyes, and could smell the wonderful aroma of the coffee all ready for her to sample. Timers were a wonderful creation. Pulling a cup from the cupboard, she filled it with coffee and had it to her lips before remembering what Thomas had said the day before.

Damn it, she loved her coffee.

Then the argument she'd had with Thomas brought another bout of tears to her eyes. Stupid idiot, accusing her of putting her baby in harm's way. And damn him for not coming to her and apologizing after she'd left.

She'd waited for hours in her bed, certain he'd come by to grovel. And when she'd fallen asleep, then woken hours later, realizing he still hadn't come by, she'd broken down into tears.

Dumping the coffee into the sink, Cassie moved to the fridge. Well there was no damn way she was going to drink milk. There were other ways of getting her calcium intake that didn't involve choking down some fluid a cow expelled.

Discovery in Passion

Shuddering, she pulled out the bottle of orange juice instead. Since she wasn't sure her stomach would accept much more than the juice, she sipped it slowly as she wandered into the living room. When she saw Thomas and Vic walking across the street, her heart ached to be with him.

He was so big, so handsome, so rugged and a complete idiot for making her cry.

~

"I barely even know the woman," Thomas grumbled as they walked up the steps to Mrs. Holloway's house.

"You don't have to be best buds; just knowing of each other will be handy. It would help if you stopped looking so sour."

"I look sour because I'm in a foul mood."

"Well, pull the smile out of storage and dust it off because I don't want you scaring the nice old lady away." Lifting his hand, Vic rang the bell.

He didn't want to be here in the first place, what he wanted was to march over to Cassie's and straighten things out. And he knew Vic was giving him a line. Vic could just as easily question the woman without his presence. And since when had his friend become so knowledgeable about relationships. Vic never had one long enough to qualify him as Mr. Know-It-All.

When an elderly woman dressed in a bright orange dress and a kerchief of green on her head answered the door, Thomas put his thoughts on hold.

"Good morning, Mrs. Holloway. My name is Sergeant Victor Davis, and I work for the RCMP."

"Bravo for you."

Seemed like he wasn't the only one in a foul mood today, Thomas thought.

"I have a few questions to ask you; would it be okay if we came in?"

"We?" She peered around Vic, then smiled. "Well, hello there, Tommy."

"Tommy?" Vic whispered and received an elbow to the side from Thomas.

"My, you're looking fresh today. I couldn't help but notice your vegetable garden is doing remarkably well this year," Mrs. Holloway spoke, still keeping her eyes on Thomas.

"Yes, it is. I've been lucky with the weather this year. I'll be going through it today; I'll be sure to make up a basket of fresh vegetables for you."

"Aren't you the sweetest boy." Her eyes shifted back to Vic. "What are you doing with the likes of him?"

"He's an old and dear friend, Mrs. Holloway. Could we come in? It really is important." Since he was here, he might as well help Vic.

She stepped aside with a nod, and Vic whispered his thanks to Thomas, albeit a bit sarcastic. "Thank you, Tommy."

"Bite me," Thomas growled under his breath.

"What a lovely home you have here, Mrs. Holloway. How long have you lived here?" Vic asked, sending a smirk at Thomas as they followed the elderly woman into a sitting room that looked like every typical elderly woman's room.

Cluttered with knick knacks.

"Came here in 1965 when I married my dear sweet husband, Ben—God rest his soul."

"Wow, that's a long time. Did you and Mr. Holloway have any children?" He sat down in a faded floral chair and pulled out his note pad and pen.

"We have seven wonderful children who have given us twenty-one grandchildren and five great-grandchildren."

"Big family."

"Mr. Holloway and I loved our quality time." She winked at both Thomas and Vic.

Vic nodded and continued, "You lived here back in 1974 when the Talbots were killed?"

Discovery in Passion

"I sure did." She clucked her tongue. "Sad, very sad."

"How well do you remember that day?"

"My mind is perfectly clear, young man," she chastised.

"Can you tell me what you remember from that day?"

"No."

Vic's brow lifted. "No, you can't remember what happened that day?"

"No."

"But you just said your mind was perfectly clear."

"It is perfectly clear."

"Then why is it you can't remember that day?"

"I remember it just fine."

Vic blew out a breath. "Could you tell me what you remember?"

"No."

"Mrs. Holloway, are you saying you won't tell us what you remember?" Thomas interjected. He could see both parties becoming irritated and wanted to smooth thing out.

"Yes."

"Why not?"

"Because I like my life the way it is."

"What is that supposed to mean?" Vic inquired.

"Just that. I have stuff to do now, so if you fine boys wouldn't mind..." She stood, indicating she was through with them.

"Are you afraid of someone, Mrs. Holloway?" Vic asked sincerely. She simply gave him a bland look before walking to the door.

"It was nice of you to pop by, Tommy. I'll look forward to those vegetables."

"She didn't trust me," Vic stated as the door closed at his back.

"And your first clue was...?"

"Which leads me to think she doesn't trust cops." He continued as if Thomas hadn't made his snide comment.

173

"An interesting development." He rubbed his hands together, smiling deviously. "I do love a good mystery. Where do you think you're going?" he asked when Thomas veered to his left.

"I've given her enough time."

"Obviously you haven't had enough because you're still hostile. Trust me, Tom; she'll knock you flat on your ass if you barge in there with demands."

"Then I'll get right back up again." Instead of going in the front door, Thomas took the path that led around to the back. When he spotted Cassie heading to the garage, he called out to her. "Wait up."

"I have to go to work," she called back.

"Cassie."

"I refuse to talk to you until you come to your senses." She waved him off, entering her garage and shutting the door behind her.

"I told you, she still needs time." Vic reminded, placing a hand on his friend's shoulder. "Wanna go for a drink?"

"It's nine in the morning, Vic." Grunting, Thomas headed to his own yard. She couldn't avoid him forever.

"Never too early for a drink," he muttered, heading back to the street. "I'll catch you later."

"Where are you going?"

"Thought I would do an impromptu inspection of the local law." Waving to Thomas, Vic headed to his rental car.

Thomas let out a long breath and slammed the gate as he entered his yard. Wasn't today just starting out dandy.

Chapter 27

"Oh, you are such a wonderful dear, Tommy. These vegetables look absolutely scrumptious. Come in while I put these away," Mrs. Holloway gushed.

"I have more than enough to do me and plenty more will grow before the season is up."

"I suppose so. Gives you plenty to share with your new girlfriend." She sent Thomas a wink, then walked to her kitchen.

Thomas smiled, following her. "Have you met Cassie?"

"Only with a quick wave. That girl is always on the go. Busy bee she is. Pretty, though."

He couldn't agree more. "She'll be even busier over the next few months with opening her shop." And the baby, but that he left unsaid. He wanted to wait to announce to everyone that they were having a baby until after they were engaged. Which he wanted to happen very soon.

"I heard there was going to be a new shop opening. Something about trinkets? Are you going to be helping her?"

"With what I can. She's hired two people already."

"That's nice. It's good to bring new business to the town. We could all use a change."

"I suppose that's true. There was another reason for my visit, Mrs. Holloway."

"I knew there was." She put the last of the vegetables in the crisper in the fridge, before grabbing the jug of lemonade and two glasses. "It's what you and your friend were here about earlier, right?"

"Yes. Why wouldn't you give him any information?"

"I already said why." She placed one glass on the table for Thomas, motioned for him to sit, carrying hers to the opposite side and took a chair.

"Thank you. Who's threatening you?"

"Now, if I told you that you would run right to that handsome friend of yours, and in turn, he would run right to the law. No can do."

"Neither he nor I would ever do anything to put you in danger, but if you know something that could help the investigation, well…"

"Why is this being brought up now? It's long dead and buried—no pun intended."

"Because there's been some new evidence."

"What sort of evidence?"

"The sort that leads my friend to believe the deceased was wrongly accused." When she hung her head down, Thomas knew he was on the right track. "You can trust me, Mrs. Holloway."

"It's Edna. You, I can trust. It's the law I can't."

"What if I were to promise you nothing would happen to you if you told me the truth."

"I couldn't risk it."

"No one would have to know it came from you."

"How else would you have found out?"

"My friend is a good investigator. Please, Edna."

"I'll tell you only what I feel comfortable telling you and nothing more."

"That's fair."

"Calvin Talbot was in that house a good long time after the second shot was fired."

"You knew it was a gunshot?"

"My hubby used to like to hunt, and because I loved him dearly, I would go with him. I know what a gun firing off sounds like."

"How do you know he was in the house when the second shot went off?"

"I saw him and his girl pull up as I was going into my house. It was weeding day for me," she explained.

"Then he was inside when the first shot was fired, as well?" She nodded and he continued. "Did you call the police as soon as you heard the shots?"

Discovery in Passion

"I did, and by the time they got here, the third one had gone off. I stepped outside to wait for them, and that's when I saw Calvin and his girl Betty came running out of the house. He fell on the ground, started puking and I thought he'd been hurt 'cause of all the blood on him. That's all I can say."

"You've been a big help. One more question though. You said Betty came running out with him?"

"Yes."

"Was she in the house with him when the third shot went off?"

"Yes."

"Thank you, Edna. Enjoy the vegetables."

~

There was dust, papers and Styrofoam all over the back room, and Cassie stood in the midst of it. This was her stuff, all of it, and she felt a smidgen of fear creep up into her belly. She was going to be responsible for selling this merchandise or taking the hit if nothing sold.

What if she failed? Good God, why hadn't she thought this through more? It had sounded like such a good plan, but now that she was here, well...

Her stomach rolled, and she was instantly brought back to reality. There was a little creature growing in her belly, a life she and the man she loved had created. The man she was currently pissed off at.

In a few short months, her life had taken a drastic turn. She'd bought a house—haunted house—was in the process of opening a business she knew nothing about, and she was pregnant. Dear God, dear God in heaven, what was she thinking?

She had to sit down to wait out the dizziness that her momentary panic attack had caused.

The jingle of her front door snapped her back, and, lifting her head, Cassie drew in a deep breath.

She would be fine, everything would work out perfectly. But as she headed to the front to see who had entered, her nerves were still frayed.

"Your knight in shining armor had arrived."

Cassie couldn't help but smile. Vic was such a comical character, and he knew just how to make a person smile. Or want to slug him, depending on what he said. "What the hell have you been doing? Your face is red and you look sweaty. You know you're not supposed to lift anything heavy. Sit, relax. Are you feeling okay? Any pain? Let's get your legs up. Just breathe, nice and slow."

As he dragged her to a chair, Cassie thought this was one of those moments she wanted to slug him. "I'm fine. God, you're worse than Thomas. Stop fussing over me." She slapped at his hands. "I wasn't lifting anything. The back room is dusty and—

"You shouldn't be in there if it's dusty. It's not healthy for the baby."

"It's fine. I'm fine, and how do you know so much about pregnancies?"

"My sister. She had twins her first time, and she made everyone know everything there is to know about pregnancy. Drove me up a wall, God love her. Are you sure you're okay?"

"I'm fine. Did Thomas send you to check up on me, because if he did—"

"Before you go on a rant, the answer is no. I came here on my own accord. As far as I know, he's still sulking at home."

"He's still mad?" *Good*.

"And worried. He loves you."

She let out a long breath. "I know he loves me, and I love him back. Even if he is a hardheaded fool."

"He had a tough time with his mom's illness. If he had stayed in Mississauga, I could have been of more help for him. But she wanted to go somewhere quiet, that's why he took her here. She was his world. When she died, a good part of him died with her."

"He told me about her. It's really sad." And because

Discovery in Passion

of it, her heart was softening.

"Do you know what the first thing was he bought when he got his very first check for one of his paintings?" Cassie shook her head. "Roses for his mom. Three dozen. It took up every cent he got, but he didn't care. She meant more to him than the money."

"You're going to make me cry."

"Liz—his mom's name was Elizabeth, but everyone called her Liz—was a great lady, and she knew how to keep her son in line. And he liked to push his luck with her often, but she always kept him in line. He gets his stubbornness from her. From what I can tell, you've got a stubborn streak yourself."

"Maybe a little."

Vic smiled softly. "His mother's illness was out of his control. Oh, he did everything in his power to get her the best doctors, into the best clinics, but still, the cancer had a mind of its own. He felt helpless and it nearly killed him. He came home one day to find her on her bedroom floor. He'd been too late to save her."

Cassie fought the tears burning her eyes. Now she understood why Thomas was being so possessive.

"I've never seen him love someone as much as he did his mom." When she lifted teary eyes to him, he continued, "Until you."

"See, now you've gone and done it," Cassie sniffled with her tears.

"Give him a break, Cassie. He loves you, and when Tom loves, he loves hard. He's not forcing you to do what he wants because he's stubborn; it's because he's afraid of losing another person he loves."

Leaning down, Vic kissed her head. "Go home. I think you'll want to see what's waiting for you."

~

The instant Cassie opened the back door she could smell them. But as she moved into the living room, Cassie was struck by the amount. Placed throughout the room was vase after vase of big pink roses.

Her heart in her throat, Cassie moved towards the vases and was startled when she saw Thomas sitting on her stairs.

"I wasn't sure if you liked pink. I know your parents sent you red, but I wanted something else."

She ran at him, nearly sending him backwards onto the stairs.

"Whoa, careful."

"I love you. Do you know that? I really, really love you."

He stroked her face, smiling down at her. "If I'd known a few pink roses would make you cry—"

"A few. There has to be dozens here."

"Six to be exact."

"Six?" Three more than his mother. He really did love her. "I was wrong staying mad at you." Cassie smothered him with kisses.

"Does that mean you'll move in with me?"

"After Vic leaves, yeah. I can't have sex with him in the house."

Laughing, Thomas scooped her into his arms. "Then until he leaves, we'll stay here."

"Perfect."

Chapter 28

The sun was setting with its glorious hues of orange, red and blues. A thin wisp of clouds scattered across the sky, looking incredibly menacing and dark, and Thomas thought what a wonderful painting it would make.

On the patio, the scent of grilled steak still present in the air, Thomas sat with Cassie and Vic, enjoying the cool evening. He and Vic enjoyed a cool beer, while Cassie sipped a glass of iced tea.

He hadn't felt so completely happy in a long time.

"I think I ate too much."

"You really took the eating for two to heart," Vic teased Cassie, poking at her arm and receiving a slap.

"Hey, that's the first time I've been able to eat a full meal without barfing it up right away."

"And what a nice vision to have after a wonderful meal."

"Give me a break. I'm sure you've seen and heard worse in your line of work."

"Oh, yeah, blood and guts I can handle, maybe even a missing limb, someone's eyeball rolling on the ground, but mention barf and I'm a goner."

"Thanks, Vic, I *was* feeling good." Cassie laid a hand on her belly.

"I went back to talk to Mrs. Holloway after you left this morning," Thomas interjected, placing his hand on Cassie's belly, rubbing it in tiny circles to calm it down.

"That's why I love him." She beamed.

"It's what made me fall in love with him, too. So what did she say to you?" Pulling a cigarette from his shirt pocket, Vic lit the tip.

"If I picked up the clues correctly, she's been threatened by the law," Thomas supplied.

"No shit. Wow, you should become a cop, Tom."

"You want to hear this or not?" When Vic held his hands out indicating for him to carry on, Thomas proceeded. "She knew they were gunshots and not a car backfiring. Her husband was an avid hunter. She knew guns."

"Okay, and…"

"Don't flick the ashes on the patio," Thomas chastised Vic, then narrowed his eyes when Vic downed his beer, and with a snide smile flicked the ashes into the empty bottle. "She told me that Calvin was in the house a long time before the third gunshot went off. He was in the house for all three."

"Get out!"

Thomas nodded to Cassie and continued. "And Betty was in the house with him."

"I knew the wife knew more than she led on," Vic added.

"Edna called the cops after hearing the first shot and then stepped outside. That's when she heard the third shot and saw both Calvin and Betty run out of the house shortly after."

Blowing out a ring of smoke, Vic asked, "But if Eddie was in the house when his parents were killed, why didn't he try and stop Calvin?"

Thomas shrugged at Vic's response. "Beats me. You're the cop."

Vic inclined his head towards Cassie. "How am I supposed to know?" Cassie responded with a shrug.

"He speaks to you."

"He doesn't speak to me. He shows me, and I never see anyone but him."

"Okay, hang on." Jumping up from his chair, Vic headed inside.

"How's the tummy?" Thomas asked softly, resting his cheek on her head.

"Full." But Cassie smiled when she said it, and leaned her head on Thomas' shoulder. "Have I told you how much I love you?"

"A few times, but I never tire of it."

Discovery in Passion

"I love you." Angling her head, Cassie waited for the kiss.

Lowering his head, Thomas savored her lips in a long lazy kiss.

"Get a room," Vic groaned, stepping outside with a folder in his hands. "Let's look at the timeline and see if we can figure this out."

"You have the timeline of the murders?" Cassie asked, snuggling up against Thomas.

"I do indeed. Okay, we have the estimated time of death at twelve thirty according to Calvin. That was when he says he came by and found them. He claims to have heard the last shot go off, the one that killed Eddie."

"Why was Eddie home at that time of day?" Cassie inquired.

"Lunch?" Thomas supplied.

"Bingo. Okay, Eddie comes home for lunch and I'm guessing, finds his parents dead?"

Cassie shook her head. "No, he was home when they were killed. He was upstairs in the washroom when the shots went off."

"Okay, maybe he was in cahoots with Calvin and Betty."

"I don't buy it." Cassie snuggled a little closer to Thomas.

"Why not?"

"He seems genuinely surprised when the shots go off. And when he races down the stairs, he's in shock. 'What have you done? You killed them,'" she recited in a deeper voice.

"Okay, then Calvin had to be there already when Eddie came home for lunch. What happened between the time Eddie went up the stairs to wash up, and the first shot was fired?" Thomas asked while he ran a hand through Cassie's hair.

"That is the million dollar question," Vic responded, grabbing another beer from the cooler to his right.

"Only two people know the answer to that question," Thomas stated.

"Maybe I need to have another talk with Betty Talbot."

"Why Betty?" When Vic lit a cigarette, Thomas tilted his head. "What did you do with your last one?"

"Flushed it down the toilet. Don't worry, pal; I didn't put it out anywhere in your precious house. Betty is the weaker of the two. She'll crack easier. Do you know your girl is fast asleep?"

Thomas glanced down with a smile. "Yeah, conked out the instant I started playing with her hair. It calms her down."

"She gave me a heart attack this morning. I stopped in to see what she's doing with the shop and saw her come out of the back covered in dust. I thought she'd been lifting boxes."

"See…" Thomas grinned.

"See what?" Vic flicked the ashes into his empty bottle.

"It's infectious, wanting to protect. She told me you came by to talk some sense into her about me."

"I went to see her shop."

"Bullshit. Thanks."

"What are friends for?"

~

He felt restless. He couldn't explain it, but he simply felt the need to get up and out of bed. Kissing Cassie on the head, Thomas slid out from beside her. Pulling on his jeans, he tip-toed from the bedroom and down the stairs. Maybe it was the three beers he'd had with Vic that were keeping him awake—which was completely idiotic because beer had never made him restless before.

Maybe if he took a short walk he might rid himself of some of the restlessness.

Stepping off the last the step, he froze.

Before him in the living room were two people, one

male one female, standing a mere five feet apart, looking as alive as he was. Yet Thomas knew they were dead.

Frozen to his spot, Thomas watched as the dead came to life.

"I've treated you well. I cared for you; I help to raise you. Don't you come into my home accusing me of not caring."

"I can hear you shouting down the alley."

Thomas spun around and watched as Eddie came strolling through the dining room, smeared with grease.

"Think you guys can tune it down a few notches?"

Thomas stepped aside to let Eddie pass and could actually smell the sweat and grease as Eddie darted up the steps.

"Eddie is right. We don't need the entire neighborhood hearing about our dirty laundry." Thomas shifted his attention to Luanne as she continued to speak. *"Of course I knew. Edward told me right after it happened."* Luanne spoke to some missing individual confusing the hell out of Thomas. *"We all thought it was best you didn't know the truth."*

"You're overreacting. Let's calm down and discuss this rationally," Edward suggested. *"What are you doing? Put that down. I said put that down."*

Thomas watched while Edward fought an invisible assailant, struggling with him. Thomas jumped when the first shot rang out and saw Edward back away, his eyes wide, his hands on his belly. The blood seeped through his fingers.

"What have you done?" Luanne cried out.

Thomas jumped again when the second shot rang out and saw Luanne jerk back when the bullet hit her in the face. His stomach threatened to rise and he had to take a few deep breaths to calm himself. He watched as she dropped to her knees, then collapsed beside her husband. His heart already pounding, felt like it would burst through his chest when Eddie came racing down the steps.

"What have you done? God, you killed them."

Thomas felt the room sway as the daylight passed and the dead vanished, bringing back the night. Grabbing the wall for stability, he sat down on the bottom step and waited out the dizziness. Sitting alone in the dark, Thomas tried to comprehend what he had seen.

He'd just been a witness to murder.

Chapter 29

Kissing Cassie good bye, Thomas headed out the door to his place. She'd planned on spending the morning going over the inventory list, making sure she had everything that was supposed to have been delivered and promised Thomas she wouldn't lift anything heavier than a cup. Because they'd come to an understanding—he wouldn't worry so much as long as she promised not to do anything strenuous—he felt safe letting her go into work alone.

He planned on checking on her after he spoke with Vic, in any case.

Thomas found him out cold on the sofa, three empty beer bottles on the coffee table and a half empty one on the floor, lying on its side. Growling under his breath, Thomas walked up to his friend and not so gently booted his foot. "Wake up."

With a snort, Vic's eyes opened, then closed just as quickly. "Dead here, come back later."

"The hell I will. Get up." Grabbing Vic's leg, he gave it a hard shove off the sofa. "You sat here drinking after I left?"

Rolling his neck, Vic sat up and yawned. "I only had a few."

"Yeah, a few too many. Jesus, Vic, this place smells like a brewery." Bending down, Thomas lifted the tipped over bottle, feeling the carpet and was glad he felt no dampness. "Why the hell did you stay up drinking alone?"

"There was an oldie on the boob tube and I just got enthralled in it. Next thing I know, you wake me with a boot. Why are you here anyway and not with your honey, smooching?" He made kissy noises.

"She went to work, and I needed to talk to you." Shaking his head at the mess, Thomas began gathering empties, Vic following him.

"About what? Hey, coffee's ready. There is a God."

Grabbing a cup, Vic filled it with the strong black brew.

"I was visited by three dead victims last night." Rinsing the bottles, Thomas tucked them back in their case.

"Does Cassie know you had a foursome with a deadly trio? Ouch, watch the head," his hands came up to his head when Thomas slapped it. "Headache, you know."

"If you didn't stay up all night drinking, you wouldn't have a hangover. The senior Talbots definitely had an argument with someone—I'm assuming Calvin—before they died." Thomas sat at the table and went over everything he saw and heard with Vic. When he was done, he filled his own cup with coffee and waited for his friend's response.

"Well, this story is starting to come together."

"Yeah, but there isn't much that can be done about it without proof."

"That's the stickler isn't it?" Leaning back in his chair, Vic gave his chin a rub. "But I do have more to use when I go to Betty today."

"Want me to go with you?"

"Would you, please? I don't think I can cross the street alone." He ducked out of the way before Thomas could smack his head again. "You used to have a sense of humor."

"I have a sense of humor; it just isn't as warped as yours. I was thinking if I went with you, Betty might be more at ease. Isn't that why you wanted me to tag along when you talked with Mrs. Holloway?"

"Yeah, but mostly I wanted to keep you from traipsing over to your girlfriend's and ruining a perfectly good relationship."

"I wasn't going to ruin it, and what's with this sudden knowledge about relationships? Last girl you dated lasted three days. That does not make a relationship."

"Things change. Fine, you want to tag along, works for me. So what was it like making it with three dead people?" Thomas lurched towards Vic, fist raised, making him jump up from his seat quickly. "Aw, Jesus, Tom, that was mean. I think I'm going to hurl."

"Bathroom. And don't make a mess." With a sly smile, Thomas watched Vic hurry away. He had a sense of humor alright, and he'd just proven it.

~

An hour later, after Vic had tossed his cookies in the toilet and taken a quick shower, they headed out.

Thomas didn't feel the slightest bit sorry for him.

"You're a real bastard, Tom." Vic grumbled as Thomas pulled up to the curb.

"I did you a favor. Don't you feel better after emptying all that beer from your system?" They'd gone to town hall to talk with Betty and had been informed she was having coffee down the street.

"Not particularly," he grumbled still as they entered the coffee shop. "Aw, Jesus, does it have to be so noisy?"

The waitress was hollering at the cook, something about burning another burger, and if he didn't shape up, she was booting his sorry ass to the curb. "Suck it up baby."

Thomas laughed when Vic covered his head and winced. "She's over there, at the back." Thomas pointed to Betty then gave Vic a shove forward.

"I hate you."

"Uh huh. Go play cop."

With a sneer, Vic approached Betty's table. "Mind if we join you?"

"I...I only have fifteen minutes left," Betty stammered, her eyes cast down.

"This shouldn't take long." Vic slid into a seat across from her; Thomas followed him and watched as he worked. "I thought we'd discuss the murder that took place in the Talbot place a bit more."

"There's nothing left to discuss."

"What was the real reason you and Calvin went to

the house the day the Talbots were killed?"

"I have nothing else to say to you," Betty stated, still keeping her eyes down.

"Oh, I think you do, or maybe you would like to talk to my superiors who are responsible for me being here, asking these questions."

Betty stood abruptly. "I need to get back to work." She grabbed the bill on the table and hurried out.

"Skittish."

"And then some." Thomas leaned back, rubbing his chin. "Your superiors never sent you here, Vic."

"She doesn't know that. Scared her, though,"

"Can I get you boys anything?"

Thomas shook his head at the waitress then waited while Vic ordered a coffee. "You're not worried someone's going to go asking why you're here?"

"Not particularly, no." He smiled up at he waitress as she filled his cup. "Thank you, sweetheart." Vic took the coffee and sighed as he sipped.

"Do your superiors even know you're here doing this?"

"Nope." He lit a cigarette, blew out the smoke. "So, is Cassie moving in with you now or what?"

"After you leave. And when will that be, Victor?"

"You that eager to get rid of me, pal?"

"No, but I am eager to find out how long?"

"I have all the time in the world, my friend, all the time in the world." He pushed his cup aside as he stood. "I think I'll go talk to the staff sergeant."

"You're evading me, Vic."

"Catch you later, pal."

Thomas glared at his friend as he walked away. Something was up with him and he was going to find out what it was.

Pushing from the table, Thomas decided to go see his favorite girl.

~

Discovery in Passion

Leaning her head on the steering wheel, Cassie waited out the nausea before continuing on her way. She hoped to God this morning—correction—all day sickness, would subside soon. She'd picked up a prenatal book from the doctor and had just started on the first trimester section. And from what she'd read, she wasn't too hopeful the sickness would end soon. There had been statements in the book of women who had felt the sickness well into their sixth month.

God help her if that was true for her.

Cassie tried hard to work through the sickness, determined to plug through it and get her work done. But in the end, she'd given in and decided she needed to go home and rest. Then Thomas had shown up, surprising her and when she told him she was about to leave, he suggested he stay and finish up for her.

He was such a sweetie.

So she'd left him to finish counting the inventory at her shop and went home.

Pulling into her garage, Cassie shut off the engine, waiting out another bout of nausea before slipping from the car. She felt the first trickle of rain as she stepped from the garage and headed to the house. Pulling her keys from her purse, she inserted one into the lock, and frowned when it simply slid open.

And Thomas chastised her for not locking the doors. Well, she'd simply have to rub this one in when he returned home later.

She kicked her heels off, heading to the stairs, ready to drop face first on her bed for a few hours.

"I was hoping you would show up soon."

Cassie moved to the living room where Betty Talbot sat on the sofa, a gun pointed towards her.

"I think it's time we had a chat."

Chapter 30

For a second, Cassie feared she would lose her lunch right there where she stood. There was a gun pointed at her, held by a woman that looked like she couldn't harm a fly.

But the deadly intent Cassie saw in Betty's eyes was what made her feel sick.

Betty stood, motioned with the gun for Cassie to move closer. "Don't be shy, come on in, have a seat."

"Why are you here?" The first crack of thunder shook the house, making Cassie jump.

"I heard we were in for a nasty one today. Looks like we're getting it. We need to talk."

"About what? And why do you have a gun pointed at me?"

"Jesus, it is true what they say about blondes. They really are stupid. It's a threat, sweetie; you do know what a threat is, don't you?"

Cassie's eyes narrowed. She hated being called stupid. "Why are you here, threatening *me*, Betty?"

"I'm here to tell you to get your friend off my back."

"Vic?"

"Yeah, the blonde who thinks he's God's gift to women."

"He's only doing his job."

"Everything was fine until you came into town. You stroll in, start asking questions about the deaths that occurred here, bringing in a cop, making the town start gossiping about it all over again. It was over with; people had forgotten about it, until you came into town."

"I only wanted to know what happened here."

"It was none of your business," Betty said with an angry wave of her gun.

Cassie's heart jumped, her pulse speeding up as she watched the gun move back and forth. She didn't want to die. Clasping a hand to her belly, she thought about the unborn child in her womb. She wanted to see it come to term, see it grow up, feed it, kiss it, love it.

She wanted to be a mom.

"Eddie made it my business." Cassie found herself saying.

Betty's eyes lifted with humor. "What do you know about Eddie? You never even met him."

"Oh, but I did; I have. I've seen him quite a bit."

"Lady, you really are blond." Betty snorted. "I'll bite. Tell me about Eddie."

"He was knocked unconscious, then had a gun held to his head. Someone other than himself pulled the trigger."

~

Thomas was busy putting trinkets and glass figurines on the shelves he'd made for Cassie when Vic strolled in.

"Aren't you becoming Mr. Domestic?" Vic snickered.

"All done with your interrogation?"

"The big guy was out. I'm going to head back in a few. What are you doing?"

"Putting Cassie's merchandise on the shelves for her."

"Where is the little momma, anyway?" Vic pulled out a cigarette and Thomas cleared his throat, then shook his head no. "Fine." He tucked the pack back in his pocket.

"She went home. Wasn't feeling well."

"And left you here in charge. Did she tell you to put out these doodads?"

"No. I thought I would surprise her."

Vic snorted a laugh. "You're doing this for her?"

"Yeah. What's so funny about that?"

"Oh, man, you don't know anything about women do you. How very, very sad. Pal, let me tell you something. Women like their things in their order. They don't like men fiddling with them. Men are good for only two things: sex and money."

"She has plenty of her own money. Two point five million to be exact."

"No shit?" Thomas shrugged. "Damn, she has it all,

doesn't she? Well, then you're only good for the sex. Trust me; she won't be pleased you're setting her things out."

"I disagree. I think she'll be happy she doesn't have to do it."

"Your funeral, pal. Anyway, I'm going to head over to grill the staff sergeant now. Thought maybe you'd want to tag along, but I see you're busy playing the fool. Tell Cassie to let me know when your funeral will be and where." Vic dodged the cardboard box Thomas threw at him, laughing as he left.

~

Cassie had Betty speechless, and by that silence, she knew Betty knew the truth. Slipping her purse behind her back, Cassie stuck her hand inside and fumbled for the tiny walkman she carried with her everywhere she went. "Calvin shot everyone, including Eddie, didn't he?"

She was startled by Betty's quick whip of laughter. "That spineless wimp? He doesn't have the guts to murder anyone."

"But he was in the house when both Edward and Luanne were killed." Hoping she pressed the right button, Cassie prayed it was recording. She let out a long breath when no music started playing. She'd sacrifice the homemade tape she'd made for herself to capture a confession.

"How do you know that?" Betty asked with surprise.

"I just do."

"What the hell; why not talk about it? I plan on killing you anyway," Betty commented casually as she paced the floor. "Yeah, Calvin was in the house, and yes, he shot both Edward and Luanne, but it wasn't on purpose. He's the nervous type, always has been."

"It was an accident?" Cassie's back was starting to ache, and she longed to rest it. But she didn't dare sit down. Any chance she might get to break free, she wanted to be on her feet to attempt it. She was not going to die.

"Yeah, it was an accident. Calvin," Betty shook her head, "he was angry that day, or at least he led me to believe he was mad. I saw the hurt he tried to disguise with anger."

"Why was he hurt?" Cassie asked, inching closer to the front door.

"Oh, no no no. No trying to make a break for it." Betty waved her gun at Cassie. "I think you'd better come back into the room and take a seat. Come on now, I'm not against wounding you to get you to do what I want."

Fearful that Betty was true to her word, Cassie inched back into the room and took a seat on the sofa. She laid her purse on her lap, hoping she was getting the conversation on tape.

"Calvin was hurt because he found out that morning that the man he thought was his father wasn't really his father." Betty scratched her head with the heel of the gun as she spoke. "Seems good ole Edward had a moment of need after his brother died. And while consoling the grieving widow, ended up in her bed. Nine months later, Calvin came screaming into the world."

"Edward was Calvin's father?" Where was Thomas? Cassie thought for sure he would have come home by now to check on her.

"Right on the nose, and I didn't even have to go into all the details for you. Maybe you're not that blonde after all."

"So Calvin came here that day to confront Edward with the truth?"

"Again she's on the nose. Edward was callous about it, which only hurt Cal more. I had to get him away right after; if I hadn't, he would have blabbed it to everyone. He was a basket case. He's been haunted by that day ever since it happened."

"But not you."

"No, not me. I have more balls than he does. I love

him, don't get me wrong, but he has no balls. He only pulled the gun on Edward because he saw it in the case. He acted without thinking—which he tends to do a lot—and drew the gun on Edward. They fought and bam." She yelled it so loud it made Cassie jump. "Calvin freaked out, saw what he'd done, and when Luanne spoke, he panicked and off went the gun again. Right in her face." Betty laughed.

Cassie shuddered, felt her stomach roll. "When did Eddie come into the house?"

"He came in shortly after we got here. Five, ten minute's later maybe."

"Why didn't he try and break up the fight?"

"Eddie wasn't the type to get in between people when they were fighting. Eddie was like his mamma, squeamish and delicate. Calvin said Eddie told them to calm down, told him the neighbors could hear them, then ran upstairs to wash up."

"And when he heard the shots fired, he came downstairs. When did you come into the picture?"

"I heard the shots. I had no idea that Calvin had shot the gun. I just thought Edward had fired a shot in the air to get Calvin to leave. Edward had a sort fuse, and he loved playing with his guns. When I burst into the house through the front door, I nearly pissed myself. There was Cal, standing like a statue, the gun at his feet. I knew then I had to fix things."

"You?"

"Eddie came running down the stairs just as I came through the front door. I knew he'd tell the truth. I had no choice but to hit him over the head with Edward's steel cane by the door. It was all so fast, God, so fast."

Cassie watched Betty pace the floor in quick nervous steps. The gun in Betty's hand was all over the place, she'd wave it as she spoke; use it to scratch her head, to tap against her leg. And Cassie knew that at any moment, it could go off.

No one was coming to save her, which meant she had to save herself.

"Calvin was panicking; he wanted to run, but I knew he wouldn't get far. My daddy would only be able to do so much for him. I had to step in. I convinced Calvin to drag Eddie to his room. He did, crying like a baby the whole time. I told him to sit Eddie in the chair, lean him over the desk. I grabbed a handgun from the cabinet downstairs, raced back up the stairs and put it in Cal's hand. He was shitting, and when I told him to shoot Eddie in the head with it, he started bawling even more. Christ. I had to wipe the gun down, to make sure his prints and mine were not on it, then I placed it in Eddie's hand."

Cassie felt the bile rising in her throat. She knew what Eddie had looked like with his head blown open, and it was not a pretty sight.

"Cal already had blood on him. I pushed him towards Eddie, while I stood behind him. I didn't want any blood splatter on me, how the hell would I explain that? It wasn't easy getting Eddie's fingers on the gun, but I managed. I used his finger to pull the trigger. Calvin nearly lost it right there in the room when Eddie's head blew apart. He darted out of the room so fast I barely had time to set things up, but I managed."

"You killed Eddie."

"And I'd do it again in a heartbeat to save my Cal."

The thunder broke overhead with a viscous crack, making both Cassie and Betty jump. When the doors to the bedrooms began slamming, Cassie knew why. The ghosts were not pleased.

When the gun went off, Cassie's heart nearly leapt out of her chest.

Chapter 31

It rang in her head, plugging her ears to only the sound of her heart pounding in her chest. Cassie's heart was pounding, which meant she was alive.

Opening her eyes, Cassie saw Betty standing across from her, the gun aimed towards the stairs. Bedroom doors and cupboard doors slamming loudly through the thunder.

"What the fuck is going on?" Betty screamed above the noise.

"I don't think the spirits are happy." Betty spun on Cassie, gun pointed at her belly making her gulp in a breath.

"What the hell are you talking about?" Betty placed her hands over her ears, the gun still in one hand pressed against her skull. "God damn it, make it stop," she shouted above the noise.

"I'm afraid I can't. I don't think they'll be happy until you're put behind bars." The noise was deafening, and it was making her head throb. Cassie could only hope someone heard the gunshot and had called the police. Then again, the guy in charge *was* Betty's father.

"This is ridiculous. You're doing this," Betty said over the noise, pointing her gun at Cassie.

Her breath caught in her throat. "How am I doing this?"

"I don't know; I don't know. Stop it; stop it." Betty spun to the window at the sound of sirens. "Daddy?"

"Your daddy's here, Betty. He'll help you, just like he did ten years ago. He helped you then, didn't he?"

"Yes, yes, he'll help me out of this. He'll find a way."

~

He'd thought about what Vic had said, and Thomas decided he'd better double check with Cassie before continuing. As he pulled up his street, he saw the cop car in front of Cassie's house. Pulling the car to a stop behind

Discovery in Passion

Vic's rental, Thomas rushed from his truck.

"Stay calm, Tom."

"What the hell is going on? Why are there cops here?"

Vic took hold of Thomas. "Cassie's in the house, with Betty."

"What?"

"There was a shot fired—"

"What?" His heart leapt into his throat.

"We don't know much more."

"Cassie, oh, God, no, not Cassie."

~

"All you need to do is put the gun down, and walk out of the house and it will all be over." The doors quit banging, bringing some much needed silence to the house.

"Over?" Betty turned to Cassie. "It will never be over. Damn it; damn it all too hell. I had it all planned. I was going to make you call your friend and tell him to meet you at this old abandoned house a few miles from here, then take you for a nice ride in your car, wait until he showed up then blow both your heads off. People would simply think you'd run off together. No one would miss you."

Someone would miss her, aside from her family. Thomas would miss her. And he would work with his last breath to try and find her. Betty's plan was flawed, and it was obvious to Cassie that it hadn't been well thought out. Betty was working on nerves and that was terrifying.

"But now you can't do that because the police are here. Your best bet, Betty, would be to put the gun down and walk out of the house. I promise I won't tell anyone what was said here, just as long as you let me go."

Betty snorted, rubbed the gun along her leg. "Right, like I believe you."

"Who would believe me anyway? I'm a newcomer to town, you've lived here…"

"All my life," Betty supplied.

"Exactly. You're part of this town; I'm not. No one would listen to me. Your dad's a cop. No one would believe a cop's daughter could be responsible for murder. No one would believe a cop would cover it up."

"I'm an upstanding citizen."

"Yes you are."

"Still…" Lifting the gun, Betty aimed it at Cassie. "I can't just let you go."

"Please, Betty, don't do this," Cassie pleaded, teary eyed. "I'm pregnant. Please, just let me go."

"I don't think so." A clap of thunder boomed overhead, making Betty jump. Her eyes darted to her right, then went wide in shock.

Following Betty's line of vision, Cassie saw what it was that had suddenly made Betty gasp.

Before them stood three very pissed off ghosts.

~

"What the hell are you waiting for? Why aren't you doing anything?" Thomas demanded of the staff sergeant. His woman was in danger, and the damn cops were standing around twiddling their thumbs.

"What would you have us do, Mr. Healy, burst into the house?"

"My girlfriend is in that house being held hostage, and from what I've seen, you haven't done a damn thing to get her out of there." The rain began to fall heavier but Thomas ignored it as it drenched him. "Yes, burst into the damn house."

"We don't know exactly who it is being held hostage."

Outraged, Thomas got right into the sergeant's face. "Well, Cassie certainly isn't the villain here."

"Tom, Tom. Come on, big guy, you want to step down now. Cassie wouldn't like having to bail you out of jail." Taking Thomas by the arm, Vic dragged him off.

"He has some damn nerve accusing Cassie of being

the criminal," Thomas grunted, sending the sergeant a heated glare.

"He doesn't have the facts. Don't look at me like that; I'm not siding with him."

"I'm going in to get her."

"What? No fucking way. Have you lost your mind?" Vic dragged Thomas further away from the crowd. "Okay, now that we're out of ear shot, I'm going with you."

"Got a weapon?"

"Never leave home without it." Reaching behind his jacket, Vic showed Thomas his weapon. "I'd rather not have to use it. Now, how are we going to get in without dumb and dumber seeing us?"

"They don't have the back secured. We go into my place from the front door and exit the back, hop the fence and go in through the back."

"It's not as easy as that. We need to scope things out. I'm not rushing into the house and have that crazy woman firing off her weapon. We need a plan."

~

Cassie had never seen a dead person up close before. Her grandfather had requested to be cremated directly after his death and had wanted no one but his wife to view him. And every time she'd seen Eddie, he'd been motionless. Seeing a dead person on the TV or in a movie was a completely different matter.

Standing a few feet away was something else entirely Cassie thought she could actually smell the blood that seeped from their wounds, and it made her stomach roll.

"What the hell is this?" Betty cried out.

Shaking herself clear, Cassie looked at Betty, who stood like a statue frozen to her spot, her eyes wide in horror. "The dead seeking justice."

"This can't be. They're dead." Betty said in a shaky tone as she backed up.

"You're right. I wonder how they got that way. Oh,

wait, you and Calvin did it." What the hell was she doing, antagonizing a killer?

"I didn't kill them all. Calvin killed Ed and Lua."

"You coerced Calvin to cover it up. You had your father cover it up. You've been in control all these years. It all comes down to you, Betty." Shifting closer to the doorway, Cassie watched as the dead moved towards Betty, cornering her. "And now they want you to pay."

"No, no stop. Stop!" Lifting her gun, Betty began firing.

~

Both Thomas and Vic ducked when the shots rang out, and when Thomas stood, Vic grabbed his arm and yanked him back down.

"What the hell are you doing?"

"I'm going in."

"You have no idea where Betty is, where the shots are coming from."

"I don't give a damn." Jumping up, Thomas ran for the door like a bull on a rampage, and with his shoulder, he broke the back door open with a crack.

~

Cassie ducked down, covering her ears, as the shots rang out around her. Glass shattered, someone screamed—maybe it was her—and she felt something warm slide down her cheek.

The sounds all began to swirl into one, right before it all went black.

Chapter 32

The door flew open with a loud crack, then hung on one hinge as Thomas burst through. From the sound of the shots, he determined they were coming from the living room. Ducking down, he crawled towards the doorway, easing his way along the floor.

"Cassie? Cass?" Thomas called out above the noise.

"Keep your ass down. Jesus, Tom." Moving in beside him, Vic had his weapon drawn. "This is Sergeant Davis. I order you to drop your weapon and stand down." He breathed a sigh of relief when the shots stopped.

"Stay away from me. Stop, leave me alone," Betty pleaded

"Step away from your weapon." Vic ordered.

"Leave me alone." Betty's sobbed.

"I'm going in." Thomas had enough waiting, Cassie needed him now.

"Tom, wait!"

Ignoring Vic, Thomas darted into the room, his eyes searching for Cassie.

"God damn it." Lifting to his feet, Vic stepped into the room, blocking his friend, his weapon raised.

Both he and Thomas stood frozen at the scene before them.

"Please, leave me alone. I'm sorry, I…I…love Cal, I couldn't live without him. I can't live without him. I only wanted to protect him."

The dead stood before Betty, crowding her into the corner. It was a scene Thomas would never forget. He could actually see the brain matter the bullet hadn't ripped apart in Eddie's skull. And the blood covering both Edward and Luanne Talbot smelt as fresh as if they had just been shot.

Tearing his eyes from the dead, Thomas searched for Cassie.

"Drop your weapon, Betty, and step away," Vic

ordered, his weapon ready.

Seeing Cassie on the floor by the sofa, his heart nearly leapt from his chest. "Cassie." Running towards her, Thomas just made it to her when the front door burst open. Diving over her, he covered her in protection.

He'd die before he let anything happen to her.

"Drop your weapon."

The torrent of gunfire around him rang out like cannons. Curling over his love, Thomas prayed they all made it out alive. When the guns silenced, the only sound he heard was his own breath.

"Tom, you okay?" Vic called out.

"Yeah."

"Cassie?"

His heart in his throat, Thomas lifted off of her and saw the blood on her face. "She's injured."

"Call the paramedics. Call the damn paramedics," Vic demanded.

Sitting up, Thomas saw Betty on the floor near the corner, blood seeping from her chest. Vic kicked the gun aside that had fallen from her hand, then knelt to check for a pulse.

"She's gone."

And so were the dead.

"Betty. Oh, God, Betty." Her father rushed to her side, weeping,

"Don't touch her," Vic ordered. "Where are the paramedics?"

"Thomas," Cassie murmured.

"Right here, baby." Thomas was never more relieved to hear his name called. "Just lay still, baby, help is on its way."

"I'm okay...I think. What happened?"

He stopped her when she attempted to sit up, then moved to block her view. The last thing she needed was to see a corpse. "Don't worry about anything right now but staying calm. Did you fall on your belly?"

Discovery in Passion

"No." She craned her head, but he shifted in front of her. "Where is Betty—I have her confession."

"Stay down, baby, just relax. Your face is bleeding."

Her hand came up to touch her cheek. "The glass. Betty hit the mirror on the wall when she tried to shoot at the Talbots. Oh, God, Thomas, they were here, all three, and they—"

"Shh now, relax. Are the paramedics on its way?" He asked Vic.

"They've been called. How you doing there, Cassie?" Vic asked, kneeling down beside her.

"My head is throbbing, but aside from that, I feel fine. Is it over?"

"It's over."

"In my purse is a tiny tape recorder. I taped her confession."

"Aren't you a clever one. Did she hurt you?" Vic asked, checking the cut on her cheek.

Thomas squeezed her hand, she shook her head. "No. I came home, and she was waiting for me. What happened? There was so much noise."

"We'll discuss it after you're checked out. Over here boys; that one's gone." Vic called out to the paramedics.

~

Cassie insisted she didn't need to go to the hospital, but with Thomas' insistence, the paramedics had taken her in anyway. She hated doctors, but for her baby's sake Cassie went and endured the prodding and the questions.

Was she experiencing any cramping?

No.

Had she landed on her belly?

No.

When the doctor on-call had placed a device he called the Doppler instrument on her belly to listen to the heartbeat, Cassie had held her breath. And the instant she and Thomas heart that whoosh whoosh of the heart beating, both let out a huge sigh of relief.

It was the most incredible sound she had ever heard.

Then they'd sent her for an ultrasound, and she had actually bawled.

There it was, her baby, so tiny and very much alive.

Thomas had held her while they watched the tiny human being they had created, flutter about in her belly. At one point, the baby had moved its hand, and they had been certain it had waved at them.

It was the most precious thing ever.

With a tear in her eyes, Cassie spoke. "I've never seen anything as beautiful as that."

"I have." Thomas tilted her face up with his fingers. "You."

"Oh, Thomas, you're going to make me cry all over again."

"I love you, with all my heart, and when I found out you and the baby were in danger…I wanted to die."

"We're safe. See." She pointed to the ultrasound of their child.

He took her hand in his and laid them together on her belly. "I know I promised to give you space, but damn it, I just can't follow through with it. I nearly lost you both. Before I ever really had you. I'm going to stick to you like glue, and if you don't like it, well, that's tough."

"I like it." Cassie smiled up at him as he touched her face. "Watch me all you like. I was so scared in there, Thomas. I thought I was going to die, that I would never see our baby, never see you again. I want to see our child come into this world. I want to raise it together. I want to be your wife." She bit her lip, mentally chastising herself for blurting that out. What if he wasn't ready?

Tucking his hand in his jeans pocket, Thomas smiled. "It's a good thing you said that, because I was just about to myself. I want nothing more than to have you as my wife. And the sooner the better."

He took her hand in his and the instant she saw the diamond twinkle, her breath caught and the tears welled up in her eyes.

"It isn't much, but it was my mother's. She wanted me to have it, and someday, give it to the one woman that made my heart beat with love. I've carried it with me ever since the day she died. I never thought I would ever find someone who I could love with every ounce of my being, but then you walked up to the fence and I was a goner."

Cassie laughed, the tears sliding down her cheeks.

"You drive me crazy with love and make me want you with every breath I have." Taking her hand in his, he slid the ring on her finger. "And I can't wait to spend the rest of my life with you."

Epilogue

"Stop hovering, Thomas. I need to breathe."

"I'm not hovering; I'm watching you to make sure you don't lift anything too heavy."

"How can I lift anything too heavy when you've taken everything that weighs more than an ounce away from me?"

"Now you're just exaggerating. Don't lift that."

"Thomas, for Christ's sake, it's my jewelry box."

He whisked it out of her hand, frowning at her. "And it's too heavy. The doctor told you to relax for the next two weeks, and it's only been one and you're up and running all over the place."

"I'm packing my things so I can move in with you."

"And I told you I would do it."

"I wanted to do it."

"Ah, the sound of love in the air is so soothing," Vic joked, entering Cassie's bedroom. "Wow, you wear that to bed?" He stroked a hand along a fine black lace negligee, then yelped when Thomas smacked his hand away.

"Oh, no, sweetie, I only wear that to seduce Thomas to bed. Normally, I wear nothing to sleep."

Vic swallowed hard, staring at her a few moments. "That was cruel."

"I know." She laughed, lifting the negligee and tucked it in the box beside the bed.

"I thought I asked you to be here an hour ago to help?" Thomas berated his friend.

"You are a lucky bastard, Tom. I couldn't get away. You are now looking at the new staff sergeant of the F-Division." Vic preened, hooking his thumbs in the belt loops on his jeans.

"Are you kidding me?" Cassie asked.

"Complete truth." Vic lifted a silky pair of panties and this time received a slap from Cassie.

"How did that come about?" Thomas wanted to know, shooting his friend a nasty glare.

"The entire division is under investigation and on suspension. They needed someone to head the division, and yours truly got the job."

"Welcome to town, Vic." Cassie kissed his cheek. "Congratulations."

"Thanks, sweetie."

"Congratulations, Victor." Taking his hand, Thomas pulled Vic in for a strong hug and a slap on his back. "It'll be nice to have you around again."

"I thought so, too; plus, I had to stick around to see this kid pop out." He patted Cassie's belly playfully.

"So what happens to Calvin and Sergeant Hopkins now?"

"They'll be doing major time for the murder and cover up of the Talbot case. Hopkins is feeling the burden of having fired the fatal shot that killed his daughter. I'd feel for the guy if he wasn't such a bastard."

"I never would have thought it was Betty who killed Eddie." It was still hard for her to believe it all.

"It's always the quiet ones," Vic added, dropping down on Cassie's bed. "I had a feeling she knew more than she was letting on about but I have to admit, I never would have pictured her as the gun-toting super villain."

"I was sure she was going to kill me."

"She had every intention of it. Thank God for nosy neighbors."

"Mrs. Holloway came through again. I sent her flowers," Thomas added with a kiss to the top of Cassie's head.

"You're such a softy. No wonder the old lady has the hots for you," Vic teased.

"Quit being a moron, Vic."

"I'm completely serious. You should have heard her going on and on about you when I talked with her afterwards. 'That Tommy is such a sweet boy. He brought me fresh vegetables from his garden and sent me all these pretty lilies. Oh, how I love him and want to jump his big hunky bones.'" Vic laughed when Thomas threw a pillow at him.

"And who wouldn't love him? He's like a big cuddly bear." Smiling, Cassie wrapped her arms around Thomas' waist. "And if she makes a move on you, she'll have me to deal with."

"You're both so fucking funny." Thomas shook his head.

"So...when's the big day?" Vic asked, changing the subject.

"Next month."

"Wow, fast. Wait, is this a shotgun wedding? Did you knock her up, Tommy?" Dodging the book Thomas threw at him, Vic jumped off the bed, laughing. "Hey, if you're moving in with Tommy-boy, can I have this place?"

"You want to rent it?" Cassie inquired.

"No, I'll buy it off of you. Wait...are the ghosts still here?"

"Not that I've seen. I think they're finally at peace."

"Nothing like a little justice to soothe a restless soul. How much you want for it?"

"We'll negotiate it later."

"Works for me. Catch you later."

"Take a few boxes with you," Thomas called out as Vic left the room. "You okay letting this place go?"

Taking a good look around the room, Cassie nodded. "I think Granddad would understand. I'm not giving up," She lifted her head to Thomas and smiled. "I'm starting anew."

The End

About the Author:

Shiela Stewart has been writing for the better part of twenty years, pouring her heart out in words, living a fantasy through the characters she creates. It has always been a dream of hers to have her work published, a dream she has finally seen come to life.

When not writing, she is busy working on two websites for organizations she belongs to, tending to her three children and spending time with the love of her life, William.

Shiela has a deep affection for animals and it's evident in the five cats, one dog, eight fish and three turtles she owns. Aside from writing, she enjoys sketching, painting, singing and dancing, as well as stargazing, astronomy and astrology. Her favorite time of the day is sunset.

Other works by Shiela Stewart:

Kidnapped

Elizabeth Cromwell is rich, gorgeous and doesn't have a care in the world. Until she's whisked away in a van, blindfolded and gagged. Liz is helpless and completely unable to fight against her abductor. Or so he thinks.

Mackenzie Tyrell is a good man in a desperate situation. About to see all of his hopes and dreams die, Mac gets caught in a web of deceit that may become his undoing.

The plan was simple—abduct the beautiful blonde and hold her for ransom. But when the feisty Elizabeth escapes and then turns the table on Mac, all bets are off. Now he's tied up and at Liz's mercy. Was this the worst mistake Mac's ever made? Or, will the choice lead him to discover something and someone that will change his life forever?

Kidnapped by Shiela Stewart is full of suspense and steeped in sensuality. This fast-paced novel is guaranteed to hold you hostage until the very last page.

Secrets of the Dead

Jessica Coltrane is a die-hard skeptic who believes that ghosts and paranormal activity are nothing more than a figment of some poor fool's over active imagination—until she finds herself locked inside a house with the enigmatic paranormal investigator C.J. Dowling, that is.

C.J., born with the ability to see and speak to the dead, thought this would be a job like many others. Calm and self-assured, he knows his business. After all, he's been listening to the *Secrets of the Dead* since he was three. He's prepared for anything—except the smart and sexy Jessica.

Working together in close quarters, C.J. and Jessica find it's all too easy to get under one another's skin during the day. As darkness falls and the tension between them mounts, a spark is ignited. Fueled by passion they give into their desires…only C.J. and Jessica aren't alone.

As the light dawns the couple discovers they're trapped. Trapped with the ghost of a child long forgotten, an amorous entity that is threatening Jessica, and a powder keg of a spine-tingling mystery that might just be better left buried.

This is a publication of
Linden Bay Romance
WWW.LINDENBAYROMANCE.COM

Recommended Linden Bay Romance Read:

Why Should the Fire Die
by Emery Sanborne and Philippa Grey-Gerou

Embrace the fire…

For months Harvard anthropologist Morgan Gregory has been searching for a holy relic, a medallion that will allow him to translate a mysterious ancient text. But what the enigmatic professor finds in the little antiquity shop in South Boston is equally compelling—former lover Rachel Alexander and a rare painting.

Rachel Alexander has been popping in and out of Morgan's life for years. Drawn to one another's magic, consumed by mutual lust and desire, their encounters have always been sizzling. Add in a secret that will tip the balance of power between them and a wanton siren willing to seduce them both to get what she wants, and the passion becomes dangerously explosive.

Together, Morgan and Rachel follow a scavenger hunt laid out in ancient rituals and artifacts. One secret seems only to hide another, and another, until soon neither are sure of the truth or themselves. Can the couple put aside the past in time to fight for the future? Only if they can admit their burning need and control the fires within, fires that can comfort or consume them.

Turn the page for a look at

ESCAPE IN PASSION
Book Two of the Passion Series
SHIELA STEWART

Coming in January 2008
Brought to you by Linden Bay Romance

Escape in Passion

Chapter 1

Victor Davis looked into the two young faces, bloodied and bruised, and thought of the good old days when he was the young and stupid, bruised and bloody one. Now, he was the older, more responsible one. When the hell had that happened?

Three months ago, when he'd agreed to take over as staff sergeant of F-Division, the police depot in Passion, was when it had happened. It was all still sinking in. He'd come to town to help his old friend Tom and his then girlfriend, now wife, Cassie, solve a decade old murder case that had ended up unveiling a cover-up in the police department. Cassie had moved into a house where three people had been killed and was convinced it was haunted. He hadn't really believed her or Tom when they'd told him, until he'd seen it with his own eyes.

The dead had come back to seek retribution for their deaths and, in turn, had turned the town upside down.

And now he was here, trying to police a town where a good portion of the occupants hated him, another portion wasn't sure about him, and a select few who warmed up to him.

One of the bruised and bloody boys before him was a member of the We Hate Victor Davis Fan Club. Lucky him.

"Okay, let's start from the beginning."

"Get bent, pig."

Eyes narrowed, Vic leaned down into the arrogant teenager's face, lowering his voice as he spoke. "That is 'Staff Sergeant', and one more derogatory word from your mouth, Darrell, will land you a nice comfy bed in the local jail cell. Now, as I was saying. Let's start from the beginning." He straightened and stood before the two boys. "Who started the fight?"

"Fuck face did," Darrell spat.

"Like hell I did," Mitch returned.

"Watch your mouth," Vic warned Darrell, then turned his attention to Mitch, who seemed to be the more reasonable of the two. "Why don't you tell me what happened, Mitch?"

Clearing his throat, Mitch began, "I was minding my own business, waiting in line for the movie when Darrell came over and shoved me."

Vic raised only his index finger to silence Darrell when he opened his mouth. "Go on."

Shifting his feet, Mitch turned away from Darrell. "I think I said something like, 'What the hell?' Then his fist came up and slammed into my face."

"You threw a punch at me first, dick weed."

"What did I tell you about your comments, Darrell?" Eyes sternly on Darrell, Vic asked "Constable Sawyer, you talked to the witnesses?"

Standing stiffly, the constable responded. "Yes, sir, I did,"

"What did they tell you?"

Clearing his throat, Constable Sawyer began, "Witnesses said that Darrell came into the facility, shoved Mitch, then punched him in the jaw."

"They fucking lie."

"Darrell," Vic warned in a deep throated growl, "you are pushing my buttons, boy." He held his tongue when Darrell snorted in response. "Now, without resorting to name calling, tell me why you came after Mitch?"

Squaring his shoulders, Darrell spoke in the arrogant tone Vic was growing accustom to. "He fucking stole my girl."

"I did not," Mitch retorted.

"You fucking did, too. I saw you with her last night and when I confronted her about it today, she admitted you were fucking her."

"Enough. I swear to God, Darrell, if you don't watch that mouth of yours, I will lock you up. Mitch, are you seeing Darrell's girlfriend? I can't believe I'm doing this." How had he gone from investigating murders to breaking up some pimple faced teenagers fighting over a girl?

"No, sir, I am not."

"You liar." Darrell lunged at Mitch but was held firmly in place by Constable Sawyer.

"I'm not sleeping with her. She's my sister Lillie's friend," Mitch explained to Vic. "I drove her home last night, and that was it. I swear."

"Why the hell did she tell me you two fu—did it," Darryl amended when Vic shot him a warning look.

Mitch shrugged. "I don't know. Maybe you should ask her that."

"Okay, no charges have been filed. You both can go, providing you keep away from each other. I don't want to have to break you two up again because next time I might not be so nice. Got it?"

"Yes, sir," Mitch said politely.

"Whatever."

Shaking his head, Vic stepped back from Darrell. "Go home, cool down, and when you have, call your girl and see what the problem is. Stay out of trouble. Teenagers," he exclaimed to Max after Darrell finally left the building and Mitch went back to the line for the movie he'd been waiting to see. "Thank God I grew out of it."

"Yes, sir. Would you like me to write it up for you?"

The kid was always so stiff. He was barely in his mid-twenties and took his job seriously, which was a good thing. Except when you remove the uniform, you should also remove the stick up the ass. Max Sawyer rarely did.

But Vic was working on him. "Do you have plans tonight, Max?"

"No, sir."

"Well, make some, after you write up the report. I'm telling you, Max, if I don't see you with a woman soon, I'm hiring you one."

"I beg your pardon, sir?" Max asked with genuine

surprise.

"Relax, Max, I was only joking. Find someone to do something with but don't just sit alone in your apartment. See you tomorrow."

"Have a good night, sir."

Waving to Max, Vic made his way along Main Street. He was one to talk. When was the last time he'd been out on a date? The memory of the last woman he'd kissed left a sour taste in his mouth, one he had too often. One he often washed away with a cold beer or glass of gin.

Shaking off that thought, he carried on. There was a crisp chill in the air, and pulling up the collar of his regulation jacket, Vic strolled along the quiet streets he now called home. There were still some houses that were lit with Christmas lights, even though the holiday had been over for weeks now. Nineteen eighty-four had come in without much enthusiasm on Vic's behalf. He hadn't even bothered putting up a tree, much less lighting his house. There really wasn't much point when you were alone.

Tom and Cassie, his two best friends, had gone off to spend the holidays with her family in the city, then off to their honeymoon in some hot resort in Mexico. Lucky bastard, his friend was. Not only had he met the woman of his dreams, but that very woman was every man's, and boy's, wet dream. She was blonde, stacked, and had curves in all the right places. And on top of it, she was knocked up, which only made her even sexier. Who knew watching a woman blossom with child could be sexy? Yet it was for Vic.

Not that he lusted after his best friend's wife; he knew his boundaries, and he would never do anything to hurt his oldest and closest friend. But he could admit, at least to himself, that he was jealous of his friend. Tom had caught himself a real winner.

"Officer, oh, officer. I need your help."

Turning his attention to the high pitched voice, Vic

saw the elderly woman running towards him. Instinct kicked in; he prepared himself for the worst. "Is there a problem, Mrs. Dunbar?"

"Yes, yes, oh, dear, dear me."

"Just relax, Mrs. Dunbar. Take a deep breath and tell me what's wrong."

"It's Mr. Jingles, oh, Lord, he's stuck under the tree."

"Did you call for help?" Vic asked, rushing along with the woman as she led him to her house.

"I was just about to go into the house and call, but then I saw you. Thank God. You have to help him."

"Okay, just relax. Was he conscious when you left him?"

"Oh yes, and yelling his head off."

"Okay, that's good. What part of him is under the tree?" Vic pulled out his radio and was about to call in for backup when she spoke.

"His tail."

He paused not just in step, but thought as well. "Come again?"

"His tail. I heard him crying, so I went out to see where he'd gotten to, and I found him stuck under the tree."

"His tail?"

"Yes," she said with exasperation, leading him to the back of the house. "See."

One look and Vic wanted to curse out loud. "That's a cat." And like she'd said, it was screaming its head off.

"It's Mr. Jingles. I don't know how he got himself stuck to the base of the tree. You have to help him, please, officer."

Letting out a deep breath, Vic walked up to the tree. Yep, she was right, the cat was stuck and apparently not just his tail, but it looked like his butt as well. Vic couldn't help but laugh.

"This is no laughing matter, officer."

He didn't bother to correct her in regards to his rank

but did stop laughing. Or at least he did his best not to laugh. "Okay, let's see what I can do."

Biting his tongue, Vic knelt down to the cat, who looked like he was ready to shred anything that came near him. Thank God for the regulation work gloves Vic wore. He pushed some snow away from the cat to get a better look. "Well, looks like I solved this one quickly."

"What? What are you talking about?"

"Looks like Mr. Tinkles—"

"Jingles," she corrected.

"Jingles, sorry, has gotten his butt stuck on his own urine." Vic looked down at the panicked cat. "Don't you know that when it's this cold out, you shouldn't put your butt down when you're taking a leak?" he chastised the cat while he hissed and swiped his front paws at Vic.

"Can you help him?"

"I think I can. What I need you to do is go inside, run some hot water into a bucket and bring it out to me." The instant she hurried to the house, Vic let the laughter roll. How could he not find humor in the situation when the damn cat's ass was frozen to the snow because of his own piss? "See, that's where dogs are smarter. They lift their legs to pee and, therefore, prevent having their balls and ass stick to the snow."

"Here we go."

Biting his lip, Vic took the bucket of hot water from Mrs. Dunbar and knelt back down to the cat. "Now, be a good kitty and don't claw my eyes out when I free you."

"Don't hurt my baby," Mrs. Dunbar pleaded.

Nodding to her, Vic just hoped he wasn't the one that got hurt. "Here we go." Tilting the bucket, Vic began to pour the water beside the cat, in hopes it would melt the snow and release Mr. Jingles.

The cat hissed, began to claw wildly, kicking up snow in his fight to free himself.

"Mr. Jingles!" Mrs. Dunbar cried out.

Because he worried the cat would rip its balls off, Vic

placed one hand on top of his back while he poured the rest of the water. It wasn't easy holding Mr. Jingles down; the cat was large, fat but strong, and put up a good struggle. The water melted the snow which released him from the spot he was frozen to, and Vic managed to scoop up the cat with both hands before it managed to run away.

"Hold up there, big guy. Let's check you out."

"Is he alright?"

The cat fought like it was being murdered and managed to dig his claws right through the thick leather gloves Vic wore. He cursed under his breath, shifting the wiggling cat to check out his backside.

That had been a major mistake.

Mr. Jingles wiggled, Vic lost his grip and the cat lunged at him, clinging to his jacket. And if that wasn't bad enough, Mr. Jingles took one carefully aimed swipe at Vic's face and scratched him right across his left cheek.

"Son of a bitch!" He dropped Mr. Jingles, and the cat instantly ran for the house.

"Mr. Jingles," Mrs. Dunbar cried, racing to the house.

"You're welcome," Vic called out, dabbing at the fire on his cheek. "Brutal bastard," he muttered under his breath, trudging his way through the alley and away from Satan's spawn. Damn cat.

With his gloved hand, Vic covered the wound as he marched his way home. *Do someone a favor and look what you end up with.* What had his life come to? He'd resorted to freeing cats frozen to the snow because the feline was too stupid to take a piss inside when it was cold. Six months ago he'd been investigating major crimes, and now he was freeing stupid cats from the snow.

Lord, what had he been thinking?

"Well, hello, handsome."

Glancing over, Vic smiled at the beautiful blonde with big, blue eyes and replied in a sexy growl, "Well, hello yourself."

Finally, things were looking up.

Made in the USA